JOURNEY INTO SPACE

A SCIENCE MUSEUM PUZZLE BOOK

CONTENTS

INTRODUCTION

Are you ready for your mission into space? With this Science Museum book, you will embark on the major steps in an astronaut's mission, from the planning and training stages to launch day and beyond, solving space themed puzzles along the way. We've been busy packing as many space facts as we can into these pages, alongside bios of some of the most important people in the history of space exploration.

What do astronauts actually do in space? How do they live, eat and sleep? And what does the history and future of space exploration look like? At the Science Museum in London, we seek to answer those questions for the 3 million visitors that pass through our doors every year. Preserved in our collections are one-of-a-kind historical objects such as the spacesuit worn by Helen Sharman, the first Briton in space, real space food in the form of tins, pastes, and cubes, and even a space toilet from the Russian space station Mir. The museum collections also tell the story of the surprisingly long history of space travel, from 18th century gunpowder-fuelled projectiles to the real Soyuz capsule British astronaut Tim Peake travelled in on his mission to the International Space Station. But space exploration isn't all about astronauts. Uncrewed scientific missions help unlock the secrets of our universe, from distant galaxies and supernovae to our own home on planet Earth. Satellites and space telescopes enable us to see the world around us like never before. The Science Museum collects models, components and space-flown artefacts to tell the story of these scientific missions and preserve them for generations to come.

The future of the space exploration is bright. As we reach further out into the universe, seeking new knowledge and maybe even expanding from Earth to the Moon or Mars, there will be new challenges to face. A new generation of engineers, scientists, astronauts, and every role that contributes to the sector will be needed to push the boundaries of what's possible. So today you're solving the puzzles in this book on your own journey to space, but what puzzles could you be solving in the future? Could you pave the way for a real journey to space?

1.
A BRIEF HISTORY OF SPACE

Humans have always been stargazers. Astronomy as we know it today can be traced back to ancient Mesopotamia, a region in modern-day Iraq and home to the oldest recorded civilisations in the world (3100 BCE). Stone tablets have been found in the region describing the appearance of the planet Venus in the night sky, the repeating cycle of lunar eclipses, and calculations on how the length of daylight varies throughout the year.

Over the next four and a half thousand years, the field of astronomy continued to develop in different cultures all over the world, as humans sought to understand the night sky and our place in it. However, this was all done with the naked eye. It wasn't until the 17th century that we had any way of magnifying the skies above us. In 1609, the Italian astronomer Galileo Galilei constructed his own telescope and became one of the first people to use one for astronomy – previously, they had been used for applications on the ground, such as surveying and mapping. Being able to see the skies in detail like never before revolutionised what we knew about space, from the movements of planets to later discoveries like Newton's theory of gravity itself.

After observing space from the ground for thousands of years, how did we make the leap to actually exploring it? The technology for space exploration began with rockets. By the 10th century, Chinese armies were using gunpowder-filled bamboo tubes as a way of powering up arrows in battle. By the 13th century, these had developed into true rockets: flaming arrows propelled solely by their own fuel.

Rockets continued to be developed and deployed as weapons. In 1944, the German V2 rocket, the world's first long-range missile, became the first human-made object to reach space. Despite its military origins and use, the technological success of the V2 proved for the first time that space was within reach, paving the way for modern rocketry and opening up the possibility of space exploration.

Just 13 years later, the Soviet Union successfully launched *Sputnik*, the first human-made satellite and icon of the dawn of the Space Age. The United States of America was alarmed by this achievement and what it could mean for security, igniting what came to be known as the Space Race, where the Soviet Union and the US pushed their space programmes to score historic victories before the other.

One of these coveted victories was to get the first human into space. Before humans could safely be launched, space agencies sent up animals, from fruit flies and mice to dogs and chimpanzees, to discover the effects of space travel on living organisms. One of the most famous test animals was a Soviet space dog named Laika, who became the first animal to orbit Earth in 1957. While these animals paved the way for the first human in space, the experiments didn't stop. Even today, living organisms are taken to space so scientists can observe their behaviour and biological processes in different conditions.

In April 1961, the Soviet Union achieved this coveted first: Yuri Gagarin became the first human to journey to outer space. His flight only lasted 108 minutes, but in this time, he completed one full orbit around Earth. He became a national hero, touring not only the Soviet Union but also countries around the world in celebration of this remarkable achievement.

With the Space Race truly under way, the next big milestone up for grabs was to put people on the Moon. In July 1969, American astronaut Neil Armstrong announced that 'The *Eagle* has landed', as Apollo 11's lunar module touched down on the surface of the Moon.

In the 50 years since, space activity has grown even further. Now, over 70 countries have space programmes, and there are countless companies worldwide developing rockets, shuttles and satellites. We're looking further out into space than ever before, with plans of returning to the Moon and maybe even landing on Mars.

SPACE FACTS

In space, no one can hear you scream – it's true! Because space is a vacuum, there's nothing for sound waves to travel on.

As there's no atmosphere on the Moon, the footprints of all the astronauts who've been there still exist today – and will do for as long as they're left undisturbed!

Did you know that up until 2006 there were nine planets in our Solar System but now there are just eight? Pluto, discovered by astronomer Clyde W. Tombaugh in 1930, was downgraded to a dwarf planet because it's so much smaller than the others.

WATCH THE SKIES!

The ancient astronomers A to E have been watching the skies.
Which of the five has sighted the most stars?

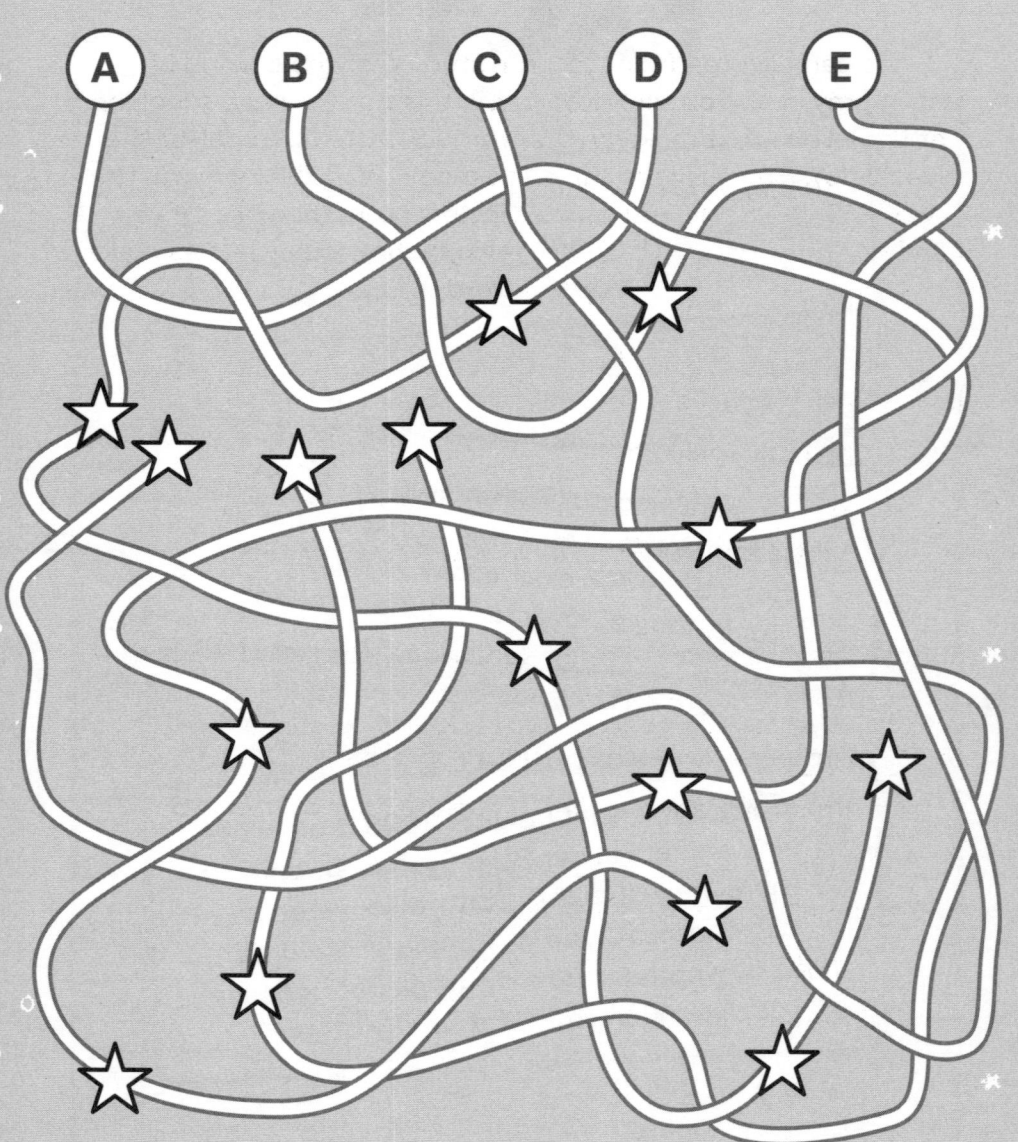

THE STUDY OF ASTRONOMY

We can't pretend that you can study the whole world of astronomy in one puzzle! However, in this puzzle, you are looking at the letters that make up the word ASTRONOMY. Look at the clues below. The answers can all be made using the letters in the word ASTRONOMY. You can use letters more than once if you need to. The number in brackets tells you how many letters make up the word.

1. It shines in the night sky (4) ____

2. A single beam of light (3) ___

3. Month of the year (3) ___

4. Another word for rocky, such as the surface of Venus (5) ____

5. Rodents that were sent into space (one was called Hector!) (4) ____

6. Place in space visited by Apollo astronauts (4) ____

7. Neil Armstrong was the first ___ on the answer to clue 6

8. A tale (5) _____

9. The fourth planet from the Sun (4) ____

10. Salad ingredient, usually red, which has been grown in space (6) _____

IN ORBIT

Orbit around the circular grid. Crack the clues and write your answers in the spaces, going from the outside to the inside of the circle. Each answer contains FOUR letters and has one letter different from the answer before it. By the time you get to answer 8, there will be one letter different from answer 1. The orbit is complete!

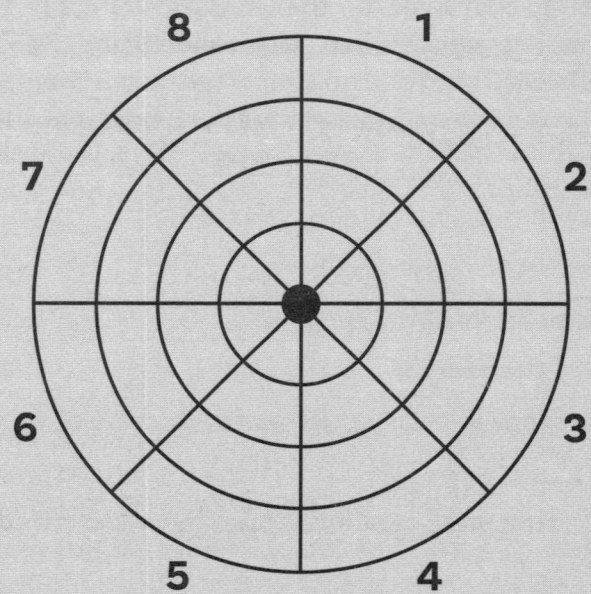

1. A competition involving speed, such as the one to conquer space ____

2. A single step in walking or running ____

3. Collection of equipment tied together ____

4. Choose ____

5. A pale red, sometimes seen in sunsets ____

6. Area of ice for training or playing certain sports ____

7. Grade or level of an army or police officer ____

8. Framework for holding or storing items ____

SPACE FACTS

Pluto takes about 248 years to orbit the Sun, meaning that it hasn't made a single complete orbit since it was discovered in 1930!

The temperature on Mercury goes from one extreme to the other, dropping to –173 °C at night from a scorching 427 °C in daytime.

Mercury and Venus are the only two planets in our Solar System that don't have any moons.

SPACE FACTS

Did you know that Venus was the focus of humanity's first interplanetary mission? *Venera 1* was launched from the former Soviet Union in February 1961, but scientists lost contact with the probe before it reached its destination.

The surface of Venus is actually hotter than Mercury, despite being further away from the Sun. Studying the extreme climate on Venus is actually helping scientists better understand the challenges we face with global warming here on Earth.

Fancy a trip to space? One day you could follow in the footsteps of Dennis Tito, the first space tourist, who visited the International Space Station in April 2001. Better start saving, though – Tito's seven-day trip to space is said to have cost him $20 million!

MAP IT OUT

The map of the heavens has changed many times. It used to be thought that our Earth was the centre of the universe and that other planets revolved around us. Try and complete this map of the skies. It is made up of four shapes; a black planet, a white planet, a black star and a white star. Each row going across, each column going down and each diagonal from corner to corner must contain each of the shapes.

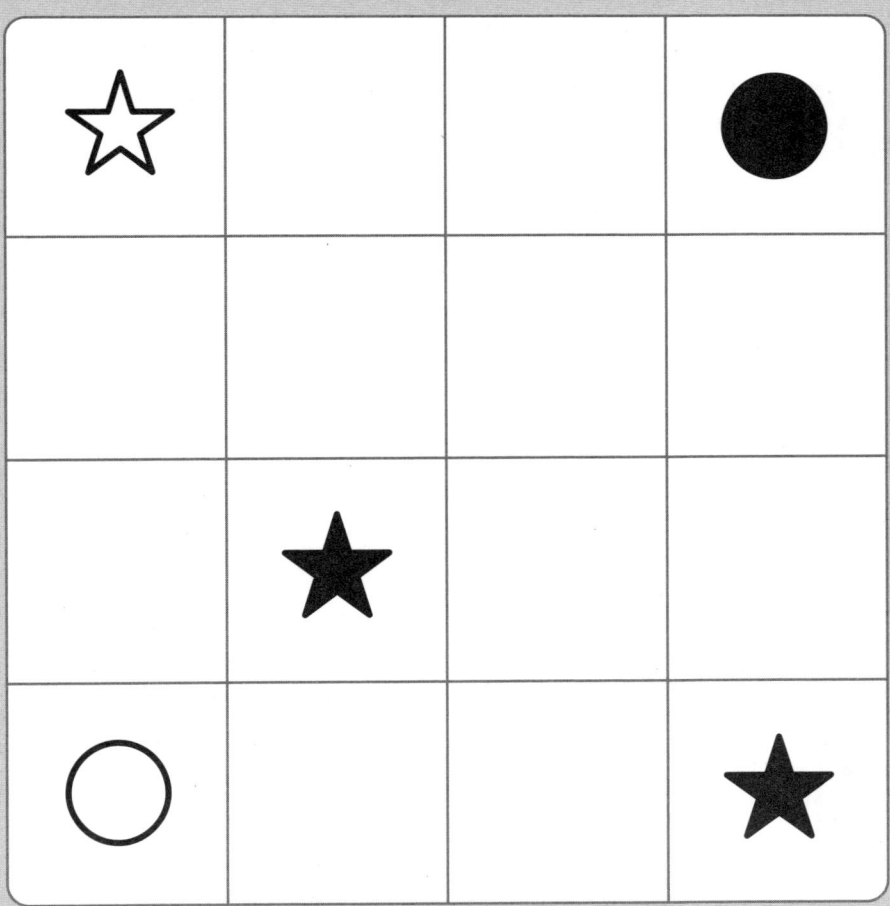

GALILEO GALILEI

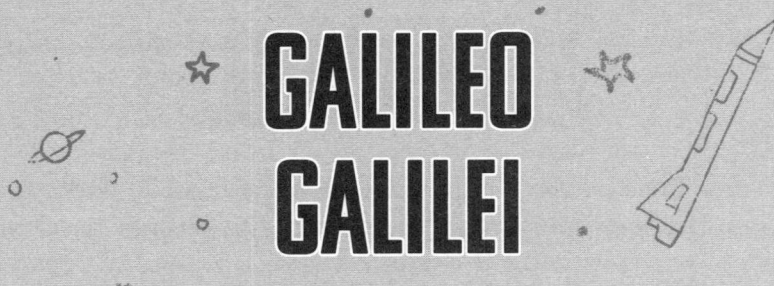

Best known simply by his first name, Galileo was an Italian astronomer, scientist and mathematician who helped shape our understanding of space and the universe around us.

Born in 1564 in the city of Pisa, Galileo's interest in astronomy would flourish after he saw Kepler's Supernova in 1604, a space phenomenon that was visible to the naked eye. This fascination with the night sky led Galileo to make his own telescopes, allowing him to look out into space with far greater detail than previously possible. As a result, Galileo found himself able to see everything from the peaks and craters of the Moon to the phases of Venus, where the planet gradually appears in increasingly more visible crescent shapes as it moves around the Sun. Incredibly, he even spotted the planet Neptune long before it was officially discovered, though he mistook it for a star at the time!

Galileo's work would prove to be controversial, however. In a time when many people believed that Earth was the centre of the universe, Galileo's studies suggested a different way of thinking: that Earth actually orbited the Sun. This theory – called Heliocentrism – is one that we now know to be true, but at the time it went against the beliefs of the Catholic Church. Galileo would be tried, found guilty of heresy and placed under house arrest simply because his work led him to disagree with the teachings of the Church.

Galileo died in 1642 at the age of 77, and it wasn't until the 18th century that a ban on publishing his books and teaching his theories was lifted, allowing others to continue his groundbreaking work. Today we credit Galileo with creating what we consider to be modern science, and his legacy of discovery lives on: the moons of Jupiter that he discovered with his telescopes are collectively referred to as the Galilean moons, and a number of spacecraft that have helped us better understand our Solar System and the universe we inhabit have been named after him.

SPACE FACTS

The oldest person ever to travel to space is actor William Shatner. Best known for his role as Captain Kirk in the TV show *Star Trek*, Shatner spent around ten minutes boldly going where no 90-year-old had gone before after taking flight on Blue Origin's *New Shepard* spacecraft in October 2021.

Mars is home to one of the largest mountains in the Solar System. Olympus Mons, a long-dormant volcano, measures 340 miles (547 kilometres) across and about 16 miles (26 kilometres) high – that's about three times as tall as Mount Everest!

The largest planet in the Solar System is Jupiter, which has a mass more than 2.5 times that of all the other planets combined!

CALENDAR CONUNDRUM

Look at the years below. They are quite significant
in a number of ways.

1609 The Italian Galileo Galilei first used a telescope to look at
the skies.

1691 Edmond Halley, after whom Halley's Comet was named,
invented a diving bell with a window.

1881 Thomas Edison and Alexander Graham Bell founded the
Oriental Telephone Company.

1961 Soviet cosmonaut Yuri Gagarin was the first man to
orbit Earth.

Can you work out the calendar conundrum? Three of those years
have something in common and one is the odd one out.

Clue: It has nothing to do with inventions or the people who were
remarkable in that year. It's all about how you look at things!

STARGAZING

For many centuries, the people on our planet have been gazing at the stars in the night sky.

How many stars are there? How many star groups - known as constellations - are there?

In this puzzle, you can see a number in the outer triangles of the star. These numbers are reached by adding together the numbers that appear in the three circles that surround the triangle.

Your star challenge is to fill in the numbers in all **12** circles. You must use the numbers 1 to 12. Use every number once, and once only. The numbers 5, 10, 7, 12 and 11 are already in place to start you off. Can you complete the quest?

HINT: Start off with the triangles where two numbers are already in place.

When you have finished, every straight line containing **FOUR** numbers will add up to the same total!

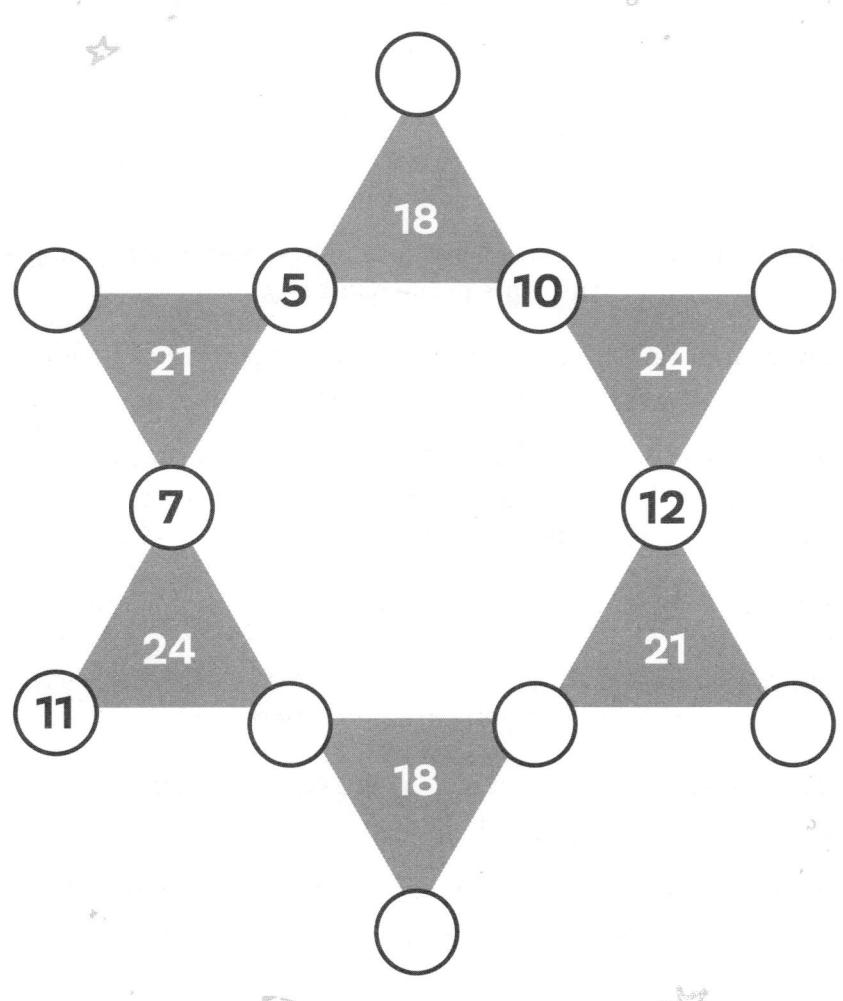

ACROSS THE UNIVERSE

For thousands of years, human beings have been fascinated by the universe, which includes planets, dwarf planets and asteroids. The names of some of these can be found hidden in the sentences below. Can you search them out by joining words or parts of words together? The first is done for you to guide you on your way.

1. The astronaut wait**s un**til it is time for him to get on board. **SUN**

2. The craft makes a turn to avoid a collision. _____

3. History recognises Gagarin's space first a real achievement. _____

4. The space agency has given us instructions as to what to do next. _____

5. Travellers wear the special suits designed for their journey. _____

6. Space experts from Mexico met several experts from other countries. _____

7. If you must tell a story about a lost visa tell it early so you can travel later. _____

8. In language, grammar sometimes seems very tricky! _____

These are the words that are hidden:

COMETS EARTH MARS SATELLITE SATURN STAR
SUN VENUS

SPACE FACTS

Jupiter is a gas giant, meaning that, unlike Earth, it is made up of various gases – mainly hydrogen and helium – rather than having a solid surface.

Saturn's rings are made up of everything from small ice and dust particles to large rocks. Scientists still don't know how or why they formed, but one theory is that they were created after two moons collided several hundred million years ago.

Astronomers guessed that Neptune existed over 20 years before they actually discovered it! They could see that something was having a gravitational effect on the planet Uranus, but it wasn't until 1846 that Neptune was finally seen by telescope.

SOLAR ECLIPSE

A solar eclipse happens when the Moon passes between Earth and the Sun, meaning the Sun is shielded from view on a small part of Earth.

These planets contain some letters that are common to all of them and look as though they are shielding each other, like during an eclipse. The letters on the planets can be rearranged to form words. There are letters on individual planets, shared letters between two planets, and the question mark in the middle needs to be filled by a letter that is in all three planets. You are looking for the names of three different things that can orbit in space.

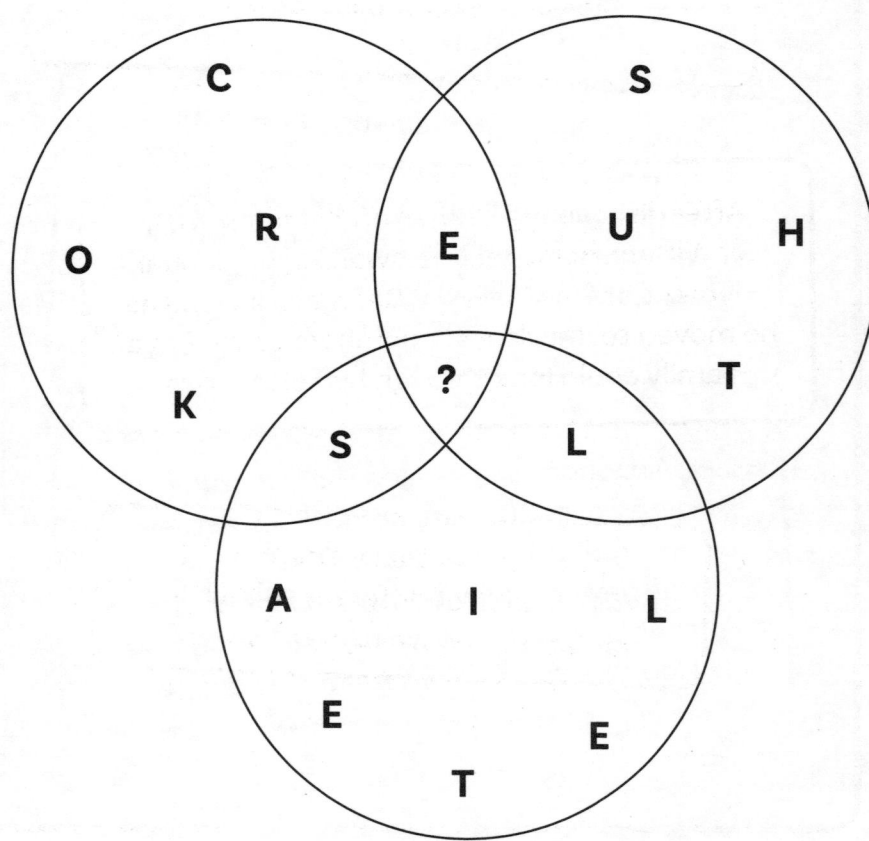

SPACE FACTS

Uranus orbits the Sun at an angle, meaning its poles enjoy 42 years of sunlight followed by 42 years of complete darkness.

After discovering Uranus on 13 March 1781, Sir William Herschel was awarded an annual payment of £200 by King George III as long as he moved to Windsor so members of the Royal Family could look through his telescopes.

Space isn't actually empty – it's full of loads of different particles, radiation, cosmic rays and gases.

SIR ISAAC NEWTON

Sir Isaac Newton, born 25 December 1642, remains one of the best known and most influential scientists to have ever lived. Long before humanity developed the technology that allowed us to travel into space, Newton developed theories that would lay the foundation for the scientists, engineers and explorers that would follow him, and explored the universe as an astronomer through the lens of his telescope.

Across a lifetime in which he was everything from a mathematician to a philosopher, an alchemist to Master of the Royal Mint, Newton is perhaps best known for his work with regards to gravity, and the popular story of him formulating this theory after an apple fell on his head while he sat beneath a tree. Whether this actually happened, or whether he simply observed an apple falling is unknown, but Newton's theory would expand far beyond the simple notion of an object falling to earth and have a huge impact on how we see the universe around us. In the years that followed, he developed his theory to include the Moon, suggesting that it was Earth's gravity that held the Moon in orbit and allowed him to predict its movements in relation to Earth and the Sun based on their gravitational effect upon it. Newton's theories were published in his book

Philosophiæ Naturalis Principia Mathematica, alongside his three laws of motion:

1. Every object moves in a straight line unless acted upon by a force.

2. Acceleration of an object is directly proportional to the net force exerted and inversely proportional to the object's mass.

3. For every action, there is an equal and opposite reaction.

These laws had a profound effect on the way in which 17th-century scientists looked at the universe and the planets in our Solar System – specifically how they move around the Sun in elliptical rather than circular orbits – and their influence and relevance continues to this day.

Newton also played a significant role in the development of the telescope that we still use today. Building on the work of earlier scientists including Galileo, in 1668 he pioneered the first working reflecting telescope that used mirrors instead of traditional lenses. This development allowed Newton to see far out into the Solar System, allowing him to observe the four Galilean moons of Jupiter and the crescent phases of Venus. This type of telescope is now known as a Newtonian telescope.

Sir Isaac Newton died in 1727, but the role he played in defining much of the science that we take for granted today cannot be underestimated.

TRUE OR FALSE?

Throughout the ages, there have been many stories about outer space. Was the Moon made of green cheese? Was there a Man in the Moon? Is Earth flat? Does the Sun disappear at night? Look at the statements below. Can you work out which are true and which are false?

1. In the 6th century the Greek philosopher Heraclitus said the Sun measured a third of a metre across.

2. Scientist Isaac Newton identified the force of gravity when an orange fell out of a tree onto his head.

3. Halley's Comet is shown on the Bayeux Tapestry, a needlework frieze made after the Battle of Hastings in 1066.

4. Greek mathematician Pythagoras claimed Earth was shaped like a sphere.

5. The world's oldest astronomical observatory is in southern England.

6. An interferometer is used to calculate how many times a person interferes and interrupts a conversation.

7. The first living creature in space was a chimpanzee.

8. Galaxy, Mars and Milky Way are the names of popcorn flavours taken into space by astronauts.

SPACE FACTS

Space is generally said to begin at the Kármán Line, which is located about 62 miles (100 kilometres) above Earth's sea level.

In the early days of the Soviet Union's space programme, cosmonauts would pee on the tyres of the bus that would take them to the launch pad. This unusual tradition was started by Yuri Gagarin, the first man in space, and even continued by Valentina Tereshkova, the first woman in space!

After her space mission, Valentina Tereshkova would marry fellow cosmonaut Andriyan Nikolayev. Their daughter Elena was the first person ever to be born to parents who had both been to space.

CO-ORDINATES

Solve the clues and write your answers reading across in the upper grid. When you have completed this grid, transfer the key-coded letters to the lower grid. The first letter you need is in E7, so slide your finger from column E down to row 7 and you will find the letter T. Write this in the lower grid. When this lower grid is complete, you will have discovered a quotation by a famous person from the early years of space travel. Column A reading down will give you his surname.

1. The month in which Gagarin made his historic space flight.

2. System used to help sea and air navigation, using radio waves.

3. Units of distance each equal to 1.6 kilometres.

4. Quickness of movement.

5. This word goes before 'down' when a spacecraft makes contact with the ground.

6. Regular path from one point to another.

7. One complete passage around Earth.

8. The direction which a compass point naturally indicates.

9. Fly without engine power.

	A	B	C	D	E
1					
2					
3					
4					
5					
6					
7					
8					
9					

E7	E5	D4		C4	A1	A9	C3	E9		E8	D2	E3

E1	B2	A8	E4	E6	D9

SPACE FACTS

Uranus was the first planet to be discovered using a telescope; all the other planets that were discovered before it had been visible to the naked eye.

Despite it being a vacuum, astronauts describe space as having a distinct smell – something quite metallic and a little like gunpowder!

Did you know a dwarf planet can be found in the asteroid belt between Mars and Jupiter? Called Ceres, it was discovered in 1801 and was initially called a planet, before later being referred to as an asteroid. In 2006 it was made the only dwarf planet in the inner Solar System. Ceres makes up about 25 per cent of the asteroid belt's total mass!

MOONSTRUCK

Moons are all different sizes (and shapes.) Which of these moon shapes has the greater diameter and is the bigger of the two? The diameter is the distance across the centre of the circle.

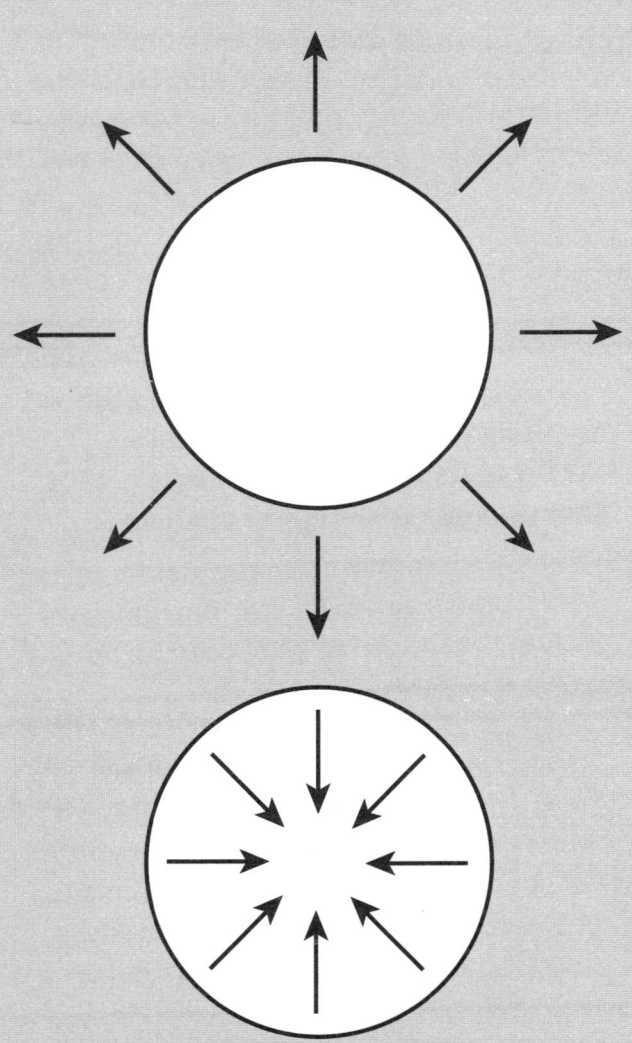

SPACE FACTS

Humans have only been sending things into space since the 1950s, but there are now over 500,000 objects in orbit of Earth – most of them considered to be 'space junk'.

The largest star found so far in the universe is a hypergiant called UY Scuti. Its radius is an incredible 1,700 times larger than that of our own Sun!

There are more stars in the sky than there are grains of sand on Earth – think about that next time you take a trip to the beach!

SPACE RACE

The Space Race was a name given to a contest between the Soviet Union and the United States of America to see who could make history in space exploration.

Below is a brief history of that race. The words in capital letters can all be found in the word search grid on the next page. Words appear as a straight line of letters. They can read forwards, across, down and diagonally bottom left to top right.

In 1945, after the end World War II, **GERMAN ENGINEER** Wernher **VON BRAUN** went to help develop America's space **PROGRAMME**.

In 1957 the Soviet Union's *SPUTNIK* 1 orbited **EARTH**. Two years later, *Sputnik* 2 launched the **DOG** named **LAIKA** into space.

In the same year, the **UNITED STATES** tried to launch *VANGUARD* but the attempt failed. In 1958 the American *EXPLORER* 1 went into **ORBIT**. In 1959 *LUNA* 2 reached the Moon but crashed into its surface.

In 1961 **YURI** Gagarin orbited Earth in *VOSTOK* 1. The same year, Alan **SHEPARD** was the first American **ASTRONAUT** in space in Mercury *FREEDOM* 7, with John Glenn being the first American to orbit the earth a year later. US President **KENNEDY** said an American would land on the Moon by the end of the decade.

Valentina **TERESHKOVA** was the first woman in space.

Russian **COSMONAUT** Alexei **LEONOV** was the first person to take a walk in space.

In 1968 three astronauts orbited the Moon in *APOLLO* 8 but did not land.

A year later, Neil **ARMSTRONG** and Buzz **ALDRIN** were the first men to **WALK** on the **MOON**.

In 1971 the **SOVIET UNION** created the first space station *SALYUT* 1, and in 1975 a United States spacecraft and Russian spacecraft **DOCKED** together in **SPACE**.

```
T E R E S H K O V A H N Q L A
S F V O S T O K L R A U S E S
O R A P O L L O P M R S P O T
V E N G I N E E R S E V U N R
I E G E R T E E R T S L T O O
E D U X I S G E A R P U N V N
T O A B M T R T S O A N I T A
U M R C K O S N T N C A K S U
N O D L L D U D O G E M E H T
I J A P E A E M O O N N N E S
O W X T R K S Y U R I L N P A
N E I B C O J E A R T H E A L
F N N O C B S M D R R E D R Y
U O D O T A G L A I K A Y D U
V P R O G R A M M E S E R X T
```

SPACE FACTS

In August 2012, *Voyager I* became the first probe to leave the Solar System and cross into interstellar space – a journey that took 35 years!

The Apollo 10 command module was named 'Charlie Brown' and the lunar module 'Snoopy' after characters from Charles M. Schulz's 'Peanuts' newspaper comic strip. 'Charlie Brown' has been on loan to the Science Museum from the Smithsonian since 1978.

Sputnik I was the first satellite put into orbit. It was launched in October 1957 by the former Soviet Union, and sent radio signals back to Earth for three weeks. *Sputnik* eventually fell back to Earth in January 1958 after completing 1,440 orbits.

2. PLANNING A MISSION

We might think of the launch of a rocket as the beginning of a mission, but it takes years of work by thousands of people to even reach the launch pad. Before the engineers and scientists get to work on designing the hardware and planning the journey, administrators and programme managers must work to set up the project and secure funding. This process can take anywhere from months (if the mission fits into an existing programme and uses existing hardware) right up to several years (if starting from scratch). Uncrewed missions like launching satellites typically take less time than crewed missions, which need to recruit and train astronauts, and then make sure they're kept safe and healthy.

The first step towards making a mission reality is to come up with a concept: its goals, key features and how it will achieve them. These concepts are often created by scientists who want to investigate something, such as an asteroid or planet. The concept is reviewed internally by the space agency or company and worked into a full proposal, laying out exactly what hardware will need to be built, what experiments will be done, and the roles and responsibilities of the team. A timeline for the mission is created, detailing when it will launch, reach its target and conduct its experiments. It's then evaluated by a panel of experts, and if it convinces them, it's given the green light to proceed.

With the initial plan in place, the mission enters the design and development phase, which involves a lot of technical detail. Mathematicians and astronomers work together to plan the route to the target, taking into account the gravity from planets and stars, and calculating the amount of energy needed to make the journey. Engineers design and test propulsion engines and the technology that will power the craft, as well as life support systems for the astronauts inside. Every detail is tested and optimised to make sure it all goes smoothly, which can take years.

For a crewed mission, the astronauts will train for at least several months. On top of their basic training, they have to be trained to use and maintain the specific equipment on a mission, and to perform the scientific experiments needed to investigate the mission objective.

Finally, after years of planning, testing and training, the mission is ready for launch.

PROJECT X

Can you solve the mystery of Project X? If you rearrange the tiles below you can find the project name.

Two clues: The first letter in the project name is I, so you have to decide if it's tile **IF** or **IS** that you must begin with.
The project title ends with a punctuation mark.

Place the letters below to make the five-word title of Project X.

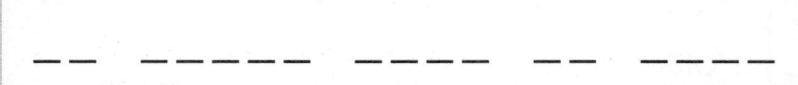

SPACE FACTS

Unlike American space capsules in which astronauts were firmly strapped in until they returned to Earth, early Soviet cosmonauts had to jump out of their spacecraft as it descended to the ground and parachute to their landing point.

While American space travellers are called 'astronauts', their Russian equivalents are known as 'cosmonauts' – but both mean almost the same thing: astronaut means 'star sailor', cosmonaut is 'space sailor'. Chinese space travellers are called taikonauts, – taken from the Chinese word *taikong* meaning 'space'.

Different types of vehicles are used in space travel: rockets propel astronauts into space; spacecraft are vehicles that operate purely in space, while space stations are orbiting places for astronauts to live and work in.

TEAMWORK

Planning a mission needs lots of skilled people who can work together as a team. Hollie, Millie and Tim are working on the same project. They all carry out different jobs and have been working on the project for different lengths of time. Can you complete the grid and work out who is doing what, and how long they have been on the project?

Read all the clues carefully, then write a tick (✓) in any square in the grid when you know two pieces of information can be linked together. Write a cross (✗) in any square when you are sure that two pieces of information cannot be linked. Whenever you write a tick, two crosses can go in the remaining squares in the row of three squares in a box. Also, two crosses can go in the remaining squares in the column of three squares in a box.

CLUES:

The scientist has worked twice as long on the project as Tim.

The administrator, who is not Hollie, has worked on the project for one year.

Millie is not an engineer, but she was involved before Hollie arrived.

	Administrator	Engineer	Scientist	Six months	One year	Two years
Hollie						
Millie						
Tim						
Six months						
One year						
Two years						

FOLLOWING INSTRUCTIONS

Start at the letter R in the top left corner. Follow the commands and move around the letter square. You will visit every letter, each one only once. Keep a note of the letters that you collect as they will form a message that applies to anyone working on a project.

Commands:
D = DOWN   **U** = UP   **R** = RIGHT   **L** = LEFT

Instructions:

Move in the direction indicated for the number of squares mentioned. To start off with command D6, you move DOWN for six squares. Then change direction and move as instructed. Remember to note down the letters in the squares as you move through them.

D6   R6   U6   L1   D5   L4   U5   R3   D4   L1   U3   L1   D3

R	A	T	Y	O	E	H
E	H	E	Y	U	I	T
M	T	D	E	H	N	L
E	N	I	K	A	F	L
M	O	N	E	V	O	A
B	I	T	A	M	R	E
E	R	T	O	S	A	V

_ _ _ _ _ _ _ _/ _ _/ _ _ _ _/ _ _ _/ _ _ _/

_ _ _ _ _ _ _ _ _ _ _ _/ _ _ _ _/ _ _ _/ _ _ _ _/

_ _ _ _ _/ _ _.

SPACE FACTS

Neptune's moon Triton orbits the planet in reverse – what is known as a retrograde orbit. It's the only moon in the Solar System to do this, and no one knows why!

The International Space Station is the largest object ever put into orbit. At 109 metres in length, it's about the same size as an American-football field.

The United Kingdom has only ever put one satellite into orbit using a British-built rocket. The *Black Arrow* was developed in the 1960s and conducted four launches before it was cancelled in 1971. You can see the final *Black Arrow* rocket on display at the Science Museum.

CODED PLANETS

This is a code puzzle. Letters in words have been replaced by numbers. Here is the code:

A = 1. B = 2. C = 3. D = 4. E = 5. F = 6. G = 7. H = 8. I = 9. J = 10. K = 11. L = 12. M = 13. N = 14. O = 15. P = 16. Q = 17. R = 18. S = 19. T = 20. U = 21. V = 22. W = 23. X = 24. Y = 25. Z = 26.

5.1.18.20.8. is EARTH, can you put the following planets into code?

When you've worked out the code for each planet, can you say which planet has the highest number when the code numbers are added together?

1. JUPITER _____

2. URANUS _____

3. NEPTUNE _____

4. MERCURY _____

5. SATURN _____

SPACE FACTS

Buzz Aldrin became the second man to walk on the Moon in 1969, but his connection to Earth's satellite began far earlier in life: his mum was called Marion Moon before she married his father!

The zero-gravity environment of space can make astronauts grow taller as the lack of gravity causes the space between their vertebrae to expand. The effects are reversed as soon as they return to Earth, however.

It took 42 launches to transport the main parts of the International Space Station into space.

ARTHUR C. CLARKE

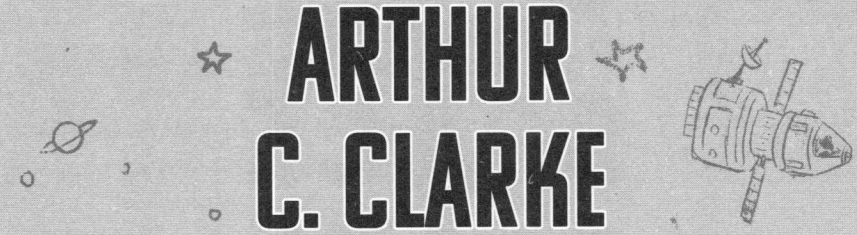

One of the most celebrated science-fiction authors of all time, Arthur C. Clarke did much to popularise interest in science throughout his lifetime and predicted many of the technologies that we take for granted in the 21st century.

Born in Somerset in December 1917, Clarke showed a keen interest in the cosmos from an early age. He enjoyed reading science-fiction stories found in American pulp magazines such as *Amazing Stories,* and looking up at the stars in the night sky from the farm he grew up on. In his teenage years, Clarke would join the Junior Astronomical Association and would contribute articles about his theories on human space exploration to its journal. Later, he would begin contributing sci-fi stories to magazines similar to the ones that had inspired him as a child.

Clarke served as a radar specialist in the Royal Air Force during World War II, but in the post-war years his interest in space would once again come to the fore. He gained first-class degrees in maths and physics from King's College in London and would go on to apply his knowledge to the *Physics Aspects* publication, where he worked as an assistant editor, and as president of the British Interplanetary Society. Beginning in the 1950s, Clarke would come to increasing prominence as a result of his non-fiction books exploring the concept of space travel; one of these works, *The Exploration of Space* (1951) would even play a part in convincing President Kennedy to support the Apollo space missions that would put humans on the moon in 1969.

Perhaps Clarke's greatest known work is his 1968 novel *2001: A Space Odyssey*, which was based on the acclaimed film he co-wrote with director Stanley Kubrick. With the publication of this book, Clarke became something of a celebrity, often called upon to appear on television as a commentator at times of special scientific interest, such as during the Apollo 11 space missions. He would even go on to host his own television series, beginning with *Arthur C. Clarke's Mysterious World* in 1980.

Throughout his lifetime, Clarke showed a remarkable talent for predicting new technologies that we take for granted today; as early as the 1950s and 60s, he accurately described telecommunication satellites, mobile phones and even the internet. He would also popularise the idea of a space elevator – a lift to space that could potentially make rocket launches redundant – a concept that had been suggested as far back as the 19th century. Although such lifts may not have come true just yet, they remain an exciting prospect for many scientists and engineers, and, alongside his many works of science-fiction and science fact, are proof that Arthur C. Clarke's legacy will endure for years to come.

ON TARGET

Scientists are often aiming for targets when carrying out their experiments. In this puzzle you must take up the challenge and have a target too, in fact there are THREE targets to work out. Make the number at the centre of each target by adding together some of the starter numbers. Choose the numbers to add together. Use as many of the starter numbers as you need. You don't need to use them all but do NOT use the same number more than once.

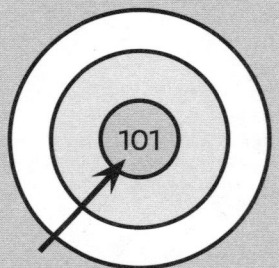

a. The target is 101. The starter numbers are: 1, 3, 25, 50, 75

_____

b. The target is 123. The starter numbers are: 6, 17, 25, 35, 50, 75

_____

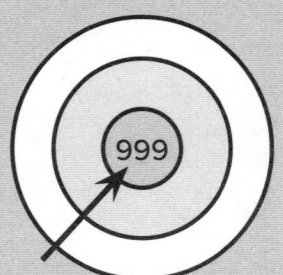

c. The target is 999. The starter numbers are: 4, 6, 20, 75, 400, 500

_____

PREPARING TO LAND

The spacecraft is nearing its destination and is preparing to land. Plot a route to orbit the planet and finally touch down on it. You cannot cross the black lines. You must move between them.

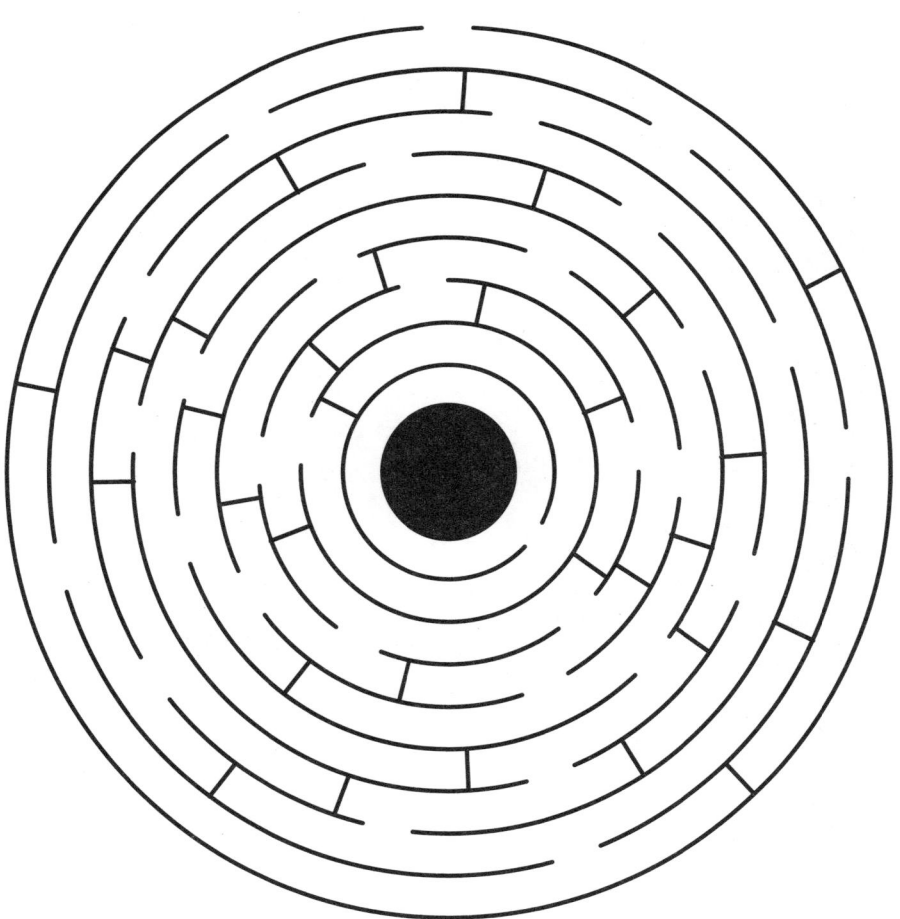

BREAK UP

Sometimes a spacecraft will break up as it re-enters Earth's atmosphere. In this puzzle it is words that have been broken up. Two words that have the same number of letters are broken up into a line of letters. The letters for each word stay in the order they appear in the line. Can you put the two words back together? We give you a clue in each case.

1. **CLSOTARUDS**

   (seen in the sky) _____ _____

2. **RSOTOCNEKS**

   (hard material seen on Earth) _____ _____

3. **CHOLOCURKS**

   (time) _____ _____

4. **CTEREAWSMS**

   (people working together) _____ _____

5. **FLOSOTORDM**

   (bad weather conditions) _____ _____

6. **JTRAOURVENEYLS**

   (on the move) _____ _____

7. **CSHAPUTSULETLE**

   (space vehicles) _____ _____

ALL SQUARE

Here's a counting and observation puzzle to tackle.

A square is a shape with four equal sides and all four corner angles the same size.

How many squares appear in the pattern?

HINT: As well as counting the small individual squares, you can combine squares together in groups to form larger squares.

ENGINEERING

Engineers and engineering are a very important part of planning a mission into space. Solve the clues below. All the answers contain letters used in the word ENGINEERING. There are spaces to show how many letters are in that answer. You can use letters more than once. In some of the answers an extra letter is needed and we give you that letter.

1. Colour of the light that says you are good to go!

   __ __ __ __ __

2. One of the shapes that surrounds Saturn

   __ __ __ __

3. Force or power that drives a spacecraft

   __ __ __ __ __ Y

4. Closer, not as far away

   __ __ A __ __ __

5. Come back into the Earth's atmosphere

   __ __-__ __ T __ __

6. Planning to create a spacecraft, or any other machine

   D __ S __ __ __ __ __ __

7. The opposite of outer

   __ __ __ __ __

8. The very start of anything

   B __ __ __ __ __ __ __ __

SPACE FACTS

The first known interstellar object to enter our Solar System was discovered on 19 October 2017. The mysterious object was named 1I/2017 U1 but also referred to as Oumuamua, which translates from Hawaiian as 'a messenger from afar arriving first'.

Halley's Comet is visible with the naked eye roughly every 74–79 years. Although named after Edmond Halley, who predicted that it would reappear above Earth in 1758, the comet is mentioned in ancient Chinese records dating back at least as far as 240 BCE!

One of Halley's Comet's most notable appearances was in 1066, the year that King Harold II died in the Battle of Hastings. The comet's appearance was believed to be an omen foretelling a terrible event – and it even appears on the Bayeux Tapestry that records the events of that fateful year!

CIRCUIT BREAKER

The circuits need a booster. Trace all the numbers along each of the lines 1, 2 and 3. In each case, add up the numbers that you come across, including the starting numbers 1, 2 and 3. The total of the numbers should be 25 to maintain full power. What three numbers are needed to boost the circuits?

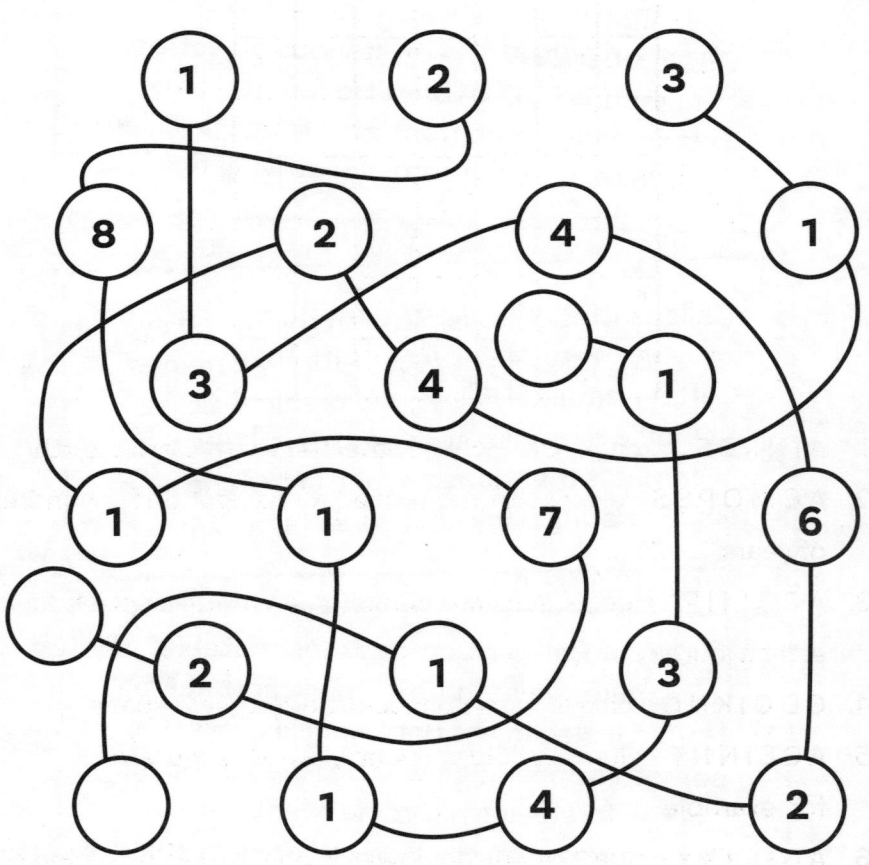

STEPS IN SPACE

In this puzzle we ask you to work out some anagrams. Anagrams are words whose letters have been jumbled up. These anagrams have been jumbled up and rewritten in alphabetical order. Can you unscramble them and write them into the grid? All words read across from left to right. We also give you a clue to help you along. When you have finished, the letters in the shaded squares will form a word linked with space exploration.

1. A I N R S S U – clue: nationality of the first man to orbit Earth.

2. A C M O P S S – clue: instrument used for navigation for hundreds of years.

3. A C C F I I P – clue: ocean where many craft made a splashdown after a journey.

4. C D G I K N O – clue: joining spacecraft together in space.

5. A C E I N N T – clue: very old, a country like Mesopotamia, for example.

6. A G I R T V Y – clue: the pull downwards on Earth as observed by Sir Isaac Newton.

7. C E I L S S U – clue: temperature scale, but not Fahrenheit!

SHUTDOWN

Time to shut the computers down. You need to key in the pass number to do this. It looks like someone reset the shutdown code and has forgotten the correct numbers. Here are attempts A to D to key the correct code. They have all failed. Can you work out the correct shutdown code?

Attempt A: None of these digits are used in the code.

Attempt B: One digit is used in the code and is in the correct place.

Attempt C: One digit is used in the code and is in the correct place.

Attempt D: One digit is used in the code but it is the wrong place.

SPACE FACTS

SpaceX was responsible for the first successful landing of a reusable rocket stage – a major step in ensuring that expensive components can be used again and again. On 21 December 2015, the first stage of a *Falcon 9* rocket was able to land vertically on solid ground around ten minutes after being launched.

Sending a rocket into Earth's orbit requires the launch vehicle to be propelled upwards at around 17,500 mph (28,000 kph), or 25 times the speed of sound!

The Space Shuttle was the very first reusable spacecraft – everything launched before it could only be used once! Although the shuttle and its two solid rocket boosters could be used multiple times, the large external fuel tank that the shuttle was mounted to would actually disintegrate after it was jettisoned.

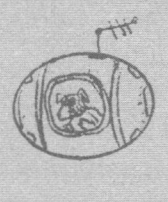

KATHERINE JOHNSON

The history of space travel is full of incredible tales of human endeavour and daring, but an astronaut's story would be nothing without the talented scientists, engineers and mission planners who support them. Mathematician Katherine Johnson was one of these incredible individuals working studiously away behind the glitz and glamour of the Space Race, calculating and analysing the flight path of US spacecraft, and playing a pivotal role in the historic Moon landings of the Apollo space programme.

Born in West Virginia in the United States in 1918, Katherine Johnson showed a remarkable talent for mathematics from a very early age, ultimately deciding after leaving college that she wanted to work as a research mathematician. In an era where opportunities for women, particularly those from an African American background, were highly limited and racial discrimination was rife, Johnson persevered and in 1953 her efforts were rewarded with a job as a 'computer' at the National Advisory Committee for Aeronautics, the precursor to NASA.

When NACA evolved into NASA (National Aeronautics and Space Administration), Johnson's career reached even greater heights, and this remarkable woman from humble backgrounds would leave a mark on almost every space mission of the 1960s, from Alan Shepard's flight as the first American in space to the historic Apollo 11 Moon landing; she even played a vital role in ensuring the safe return of the Apollo 13 crew after disaster struck their mission in April 1970. Incredibly, astronaut John Glenn requested that Johnson verify the workings of an actual electronic computer before his first mission to orbit Earth. Johnson would subsequently work on mission planning for Space Shuttle flights before retiring from NASA in 1986. In 2015, she was awarded the Presidential Medal of Freedom, the highest civilian award in the US, by President Obama.

Katherine Johnson died in February 2020 aged 101, but her legacy will live on for many years to come: through her passion for mathematics she has inspired whole generations, paving the way for women and people from minority communities to pursue successful careers in science, technology, engineering and maths. Johnson's incredible story, alongside her colleagues Mary Jackson and Dorothy Vaughan, was mmortalised in the 2016 Hollywood film *Hidden Figures*, finally bringing widespread attention to the remarkable role these talented women played in humanity's voyage to the stars.

3. TRAINING TO BE AN ASTRONAUT

In 1961, Russian cosmonaut Yuri Gagarin became the first person in space. By the end of 2023, the total number of people who have been to space reached nearly 700. This includes some high-flying pilots and space tourists, but the majority have been professional astronauts. So, how do you become a professional astronaut?

As with any job, the first step is to apply! When space agencies like the National Aeronautics and Space Administration (NASA) in the US and the European Space Agency (ESA) in Europe put out a call to recruit new astronauts, they set out their entry requirements. Most importantly, applicants need to have at least a Master's degree in a STEM subject (science, technology, engineering, mathematics) and relevant professional experience. This can be from working as a scientist, but many astronauts gain such experience by working as test pilots: highly qualified pilots who specialise in flying and evaluating new and experimental aircraft. Neil Armstrong, who became the first person to walk on the Moon in 1969, started out as a pilot and had more than 2,450 hours of flying experience before joining the space programme!

Being an astronaut is gruelling work, so to make sure they are fit and healthy for the job, all aspiring astronauts also have to undergo a medical examination. This measures things like their eyesight, blood pressure and even their height. Astronauts have to be tall enough to reach all the buttons and controls, but small enough to fit comfortably in the cramped spacecraft. This varies between agencies and missions and often depends on the spacecraft, but ESA, for example, requires astronauts to be between 153 and 190cm (5 and 6 feet) tall.

After they pass the application, interview and physical, the successful recruits begin training. It typically takes around two years to complete the basic training. This includes academic subjects such as spaceflight engineering, astronomy and electrical engineering, alongside practical skills such as languages (especially Russian, which is one of the main languages of the space sector alongside English), survival skills and even SCUBA diving. SCUBA training helps astronauts prepare for extra-vehicular activity (EVA), also known as spacewalks, as they need to be comfortable using breathing apparatus and working in a weightless environment.

This basic training gives new recruits the foundation they need to progress to specialist training. Specialist training is tailored to the mission, so astronauts can practise exactly what they'll be doing up in space. Astronauts tasked with servicing the Hubble Space Telescope, for example, trained using a model of Hubble in a 'neutral buoyancy tank', a deep pool of water like a swimming pool. In fact, in the early days of the space programme, NASA just used swimming pools until dedicated facilities were built! These allow astronauts to practise doing their job under weightless conditions, while wearing the bulky protective suits and gloves that are needed to protect them in space. However, these tanks can't completely replicate the space environment: the biggest difference is that your muscles have to work much harder to move around in water than they do in a vacuum that has no resistance. Recruits also train for any scientific experiments they'll be undertaking. Apollo astronauts, for example, were trained in geology to prepare them for collecting samples of Moon rock.

Socialising is a key part of training for a mission. The crew need to get to know each other and rehearse working as a team, with each astronaut having their own roles and responsibilities. Missions are mentally and emotionally demanding as well as physically, so astronauts also study human behaviour, communication and culture for them and their team's wellbeing.

Once an astronaut has completed their mission training, they are ready to fly...

SPACE FACTS

The rockets used in the US space programme of the 1960s had their origins in the V2 rockets built by Germany during World War II. Wernher Von Braun, designer of the V2, would go on to develop the rockets that sent the first US astronaut into space, and would eventually take humans to the Moon.

The former Soviet Union built their own reusable Space Shuttle. Four examples were built: *Buran*, which took part in the programme's only flight in November 1988; *Ptichka*, which was intended to fly the second mission; and two full-scale models that were intended for ground-based training.

The Russian Soyuz spacecraft were introduced in the 1960s, and with many improvements, modifications and variations continue to be used today. They have taken part in more space missions than any other spacecraft that has ever flown.

ALL ACTION

As part of their training, astronauts must learn lots of skills, including ways of exercising and increasing their fitness in readiness for their trip to outer space.

Look at the list of action words below then search them out in the letter grid. Words can be found in straight lines of capital letters. Words can be read forwards, backwards, up, down or any way diagonally. One word can be found three times. What is it?

ACT
ASCEND
CLIMB
DASH
DESCEND
DIVE
DOWN
FLOAT
FLY
HURRY
JOG
JUMP
LEAP
MOVE
RACE
RUN
STAND
STROLL
SWIM
TRAIN
WALK

D	H	O	O	T	E	J	T	O	S	Y	S
R	E	J	L	H	P	A	N	W	T	P	E
G	E	S	U	M	O	P	I	R	A	Y	O
H	A	N	C	L	I	M	B	I	N	L	I
U	U	M	F	E	H	U	P	A	D	E	K
R	O	R	L	E	N	J	O	N	R	A	T
R	A	Z	Y	C	D	D	I	P	U	P	R
Y	E	C	S	N	D	A	I	X	R	A	D
D	E	A	E	S	R	E	S	V	D	S	O
Z	R	C	J	T	V	I	W	H	E	M	W
L	S	T	R	O	L	L	I	P	B	O	N
A	N	D	M	A	G	S	M	I	W	S	O

INTERVIEW

To sign up for any job or type of work, you have to apply. Then there will be an interview, where a team of experts will ask you questions to see if you will suit the job and if the job will suit you.

Four nervous people are waiting for their turn to go into the interview room. There is **Li**, **Matt**, **Mila** and **Tim**. They all want to be astronauts.

If they had been interviewed in alphabetical order of their first names, then **Li** would have gone first, followed by **Matt**, then **Mila** and finally **Tim**. None of our candidates were interviewed in their alphabetical positions. So, **Li** was not first, **Matt** was not second, **Mila** was not third and **Tim** was not fourth and last.

In fact, **Tim** was interviewed directly after **Mila**. Neither was first in.

In which order were they interviewed?

NUMBER NAMES

Great news! Our four people from the INTERVIEW puzzle have all been taken on and they are now training to be astronauts.

It is decided each one should have a coded number name as identification. The four first names only use five DIFFERENT letters of the alphabet. They are A, I, L, M and T. Every letter has been given a numerical value from 1 to 5. The values stay the same throughout.

The coded number names are worked out by adding the values of the individual letters in the actual names.

T I M = 6

L I = 8

M A T T = 8

What code number is given to **MILA**?

HINT: TIM = 6. His name has three different letters. Which three different numbers total **6**?

SPACE FACTS

Fancy a workout in space? There's a gym aboard the International Space Station and astronauts exercise for around two hours each day to prevent losing muscle and bone mass in the zero-gravity environment!

NASA's mission to return to the Moon in the 21st century is named Artemis; in Greek mythology, Artemis was the twin sister of Apollo, the god of divine distance, for whom the original Moon missions were named.

Did you know there's water on the Moon? For centuries, astronomers have referred to the dark patches on the Moon's surface as oceans, but while they don't hold water like the oceans here on Earth, there are huge amounts of ice at the lunar poles.

SHAPE UP

The recruits are set a challenge to build a small robot from various parts. Which box of parts could build the robot?

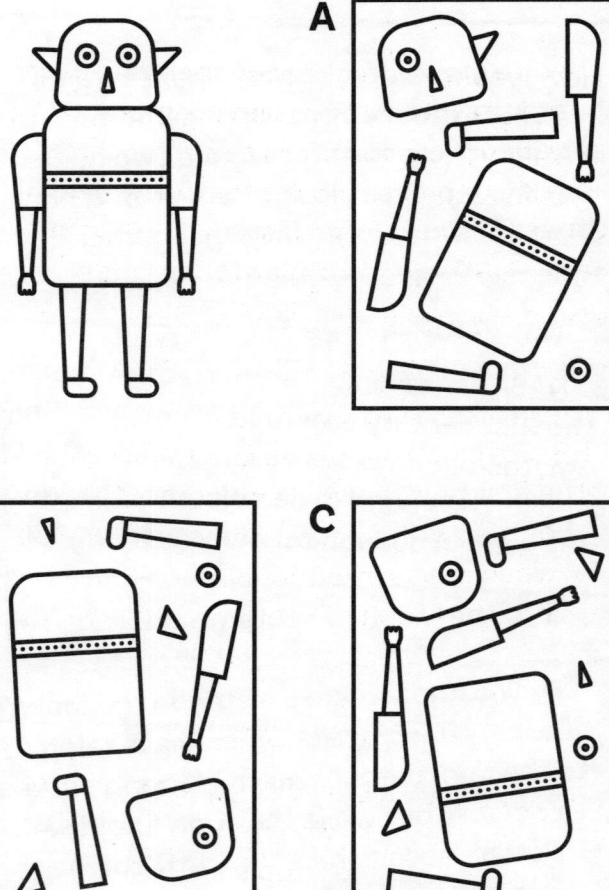

A

B

C

SPACE FACTS

How would you feel about spending over a year in space? Russian cosmonaut Valery Polyakov holds the record for having stayed in space for the longest single mission, which lasted an incredible 438 days! He was aboard the Mir space station from January 1994 to March 1995.

The Soviet space probe *Luna 2* became the first human-made object to make contact with another celestial body when it was intentionally crashed into the Moon in September 1959.

Loads of things were left on the Moon after the Apollo missions, from moon buggies and flags to photographs, tools and equipment – even bags of the astronauts' poo and wee!

JOHN GLENN

John Glenn (1921–2016) is one of the most famous names in the history of American space flight. A lifelong obsession with powered flight began early in Glenn's life when he joined his father on a flight at the age of eight. In 1941 he would earn a private pilot's licence, and when the United States entered World War II Glenn would end his college studies to join the US Army Air Corps, serving his country with distinction throughout the 1940s and 50s.

With so much experience flying aeroplanes, it was natural for Glenn to qualify as a test pilot in the mid-1950s and, in 1957, he became the first person to make a transcontinental supersonic flight. But this was just the beginning: three months after his historic flight, the Soviet Union put the *Sputnik* 1 satellite into orbit, and suddenly the US was racing to catch up. A year later, the National Air and Space Administration (NASA) was formed, and shortly thereafter Project Mercury was announced, stating America's intention to put a human being in orbit. Mercury-Atlas 6 launched on February 20, 1962, with the *Friendship* 7 space capsule carrying Glenn on three orbits around Earth in a little under five hours, in the process making him the third American and only the fifth person ever to travel to space.

Upon his return to Earth, Glenn found himself celebrated as a national hero, and with it looking unlikely that he would be selected for future space missions, he channelled his popularity into other areas, including business ventures and, eventually, politics. After two failed attempts, he was finally successful in winning a seat in the United States senate in 1976, beginning a political career that would last until the end of the 20th century.

But for all his Earth-bound work, Glenn would eventually find his way back into orbit. In the late 1990s, he argued that NASA should send an older person into space after realising that some of the difficulties that humans face as they age – such as the loss of bone density and decrease in muscle mass – are similar to what astronauts experience in a low-gravity environment. NASA agreed, and Glenn was assigned to the Space Shuttle *Discovery* as a payload specialist in October 1998, ultimately spending almost ten days in orbit – and making him at the time the oldest human being to have travelled into space.

TYPO

Reading a training manual, an instruction book, is high on the list of importance for the trainee astronauts, or ASCANs. Unfortunately, some words are spelt wrongly as they contain one wrong letter. Can you correct the sentences and put the astronauts back on the right track?

There is always excitement at the thought of gravel to outer spice in a pocket. Lumans have landed on the moor but not on cars. All astronauts need a helpful crow behind the scenes.

Some astronauts have been used to flying planks before they ventured beyond Earth. As part of their training they may live in cakes, or in showy goods. Sometimes they practise in banks full of water. They carry out vests and checks are made on their wealth. They must tear a special spit.

JIGSAW

A crossword, which is nine squares by nine squares, has been broken up into nine pieces like a jigsaw. Can you put the pieces back together again? **HINT**: The letter that needs to appear in the top left square is a **C**.

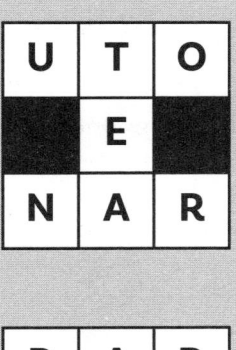

MAKING CONNECTIONS

Training allows you to develop the skill of making connections. In this puzzle we give you a word, a blank space and then another word. Your skill will be tested as you must find a word that links the two. The blank space has enough dashes to fit in the missing word.

1 SOFT(_ _ _ _)HOUSE

2. FORE(_ _ _ _)QUARTERS

3. UNDER(_ _ _ _ _)MELON

4. LIFT(_ _ _)SIDE

5. SPELLING(_ _ _ _)PILOT

6. BULLS(_ _ _)SIGHT

7. TOUCH(_ _ _ _)LOAD

8. CRASH(_ _ _ _)SLIDE

LEVELS

Being able to carry out scientific tests is an important part of training to be an astronaut. Something seems to have gone wrong with this experiment! The glass tubes, A to K, are connected to either glass 1 or glass 2. The level of liquid in the tubes should be the same as the level in the large glass to which they are linked. For example, the level in tube B should be the same as the level in glass 1. There are TWO tubes that defy science and have levels that are not the same as the feeder glasses. Can you keep on the level and discover which they are?

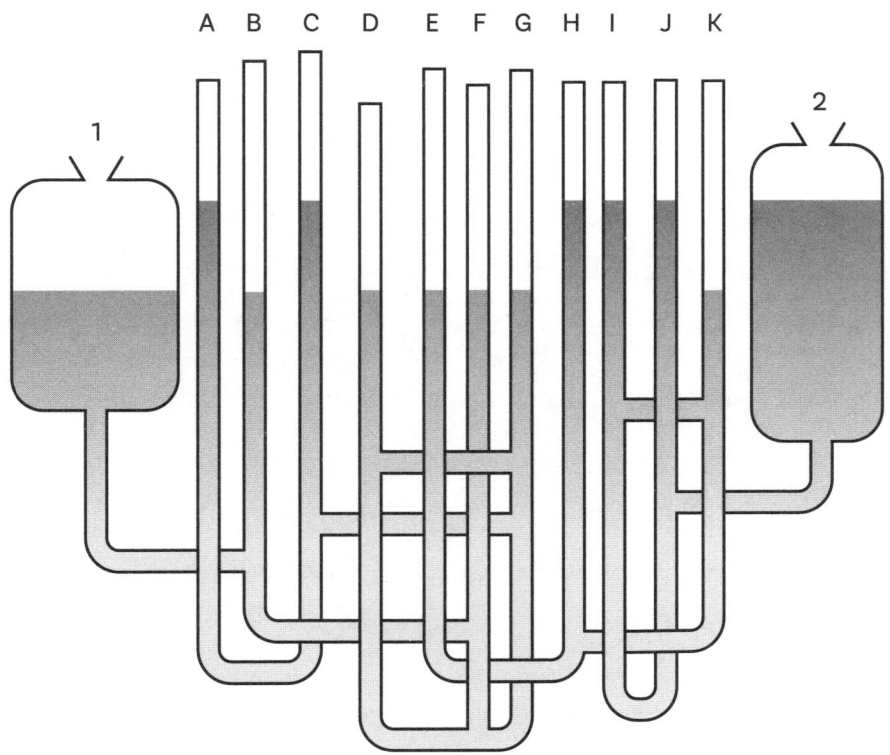

YURI GAGARIN

One of the most famous names ever associated with human space travel is Yuri Gagarin, the first human being to ever venture into space.

But for such a renowned figure, Yuri Gagarin came from incredibly humble beginnings. Born in the village of Klushino in 1934, Gagarin's early years were not easy; aged just seven his home was taken over by German soldiers during the Second World War. Young Yuri subsequently became something of a saboteur, bravely disrupting the operations of the forces occupying his village. Amid such hardship, however, it was also around this time that Gagarin's interest in aircraft was born, after a fighter plane crashed nearby.

After the war, 12 year old Yuri returned to his studies and it was here that he really began to explore his passion for aeroplanes by learning to fly light aircraft, before going on to train as a Soviet air cadet. In late November 1957, he became a lieutenant in the Soviet Air Force, and just two years later he would express interest in the Soviet Union's space programme – a decision that would not only make him the first human in space, but also catapult him to global fame.

Gagarin would undergo a comprehensive training program that involved both physical and mental exercises, and would eventually be chosen from a group of 20 men to be the first cosmonaut. On 12 April 1961, Yuri Gagarin was strapped into the *Vostok 1* spacecraft, and at 6:07am it blasted off from the Baikonur Cosmodrome, propelling him into orbit.

Though his time in space lasted just 108 minutes from the moment of launch to the time of landing, and encompassed just one orbit of Earth, Gagarin's place in history was cemented. Upon his safe return he was celebrated as national hero, was the recipient of numerous medals and awards and became a worldwide celebrity.

Gagarin would never travel into space again, but in the years after his mission he would remain closely associated with the Soviet space program, most notably as deputy training director at Star City overseeing the cosmonauts who would follow in his footsteps. Tragically, Yuri Gagarin's life would end at the age of just 34 when a plane he was piloting during a training flight crashed in March 1968. The role he played in humanity's earliest steps into space cannot be underestimated, however, nor will his name ever be forgotten.

SPACE PLACE

There is a pattern to all these groups of numbers. Can you keep the pattern going and place numbers in the empty spaces?

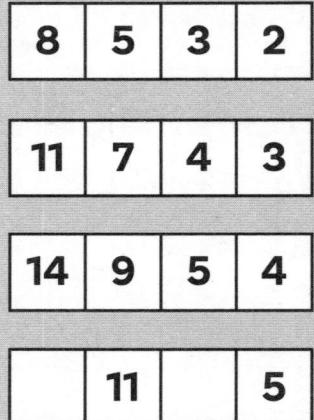

8	5	3	2

11	7	4	3

14	9	5	4

	11		5

EYE, EYE

Testing of the eyesight is part of the training to be an astronaut. In our chart of letters, you will need to see what *isn't* there. Every letter has had a single straight line removed from it. Can you work out what words are formed by the completed letters? All the words could appear on a computer screen.

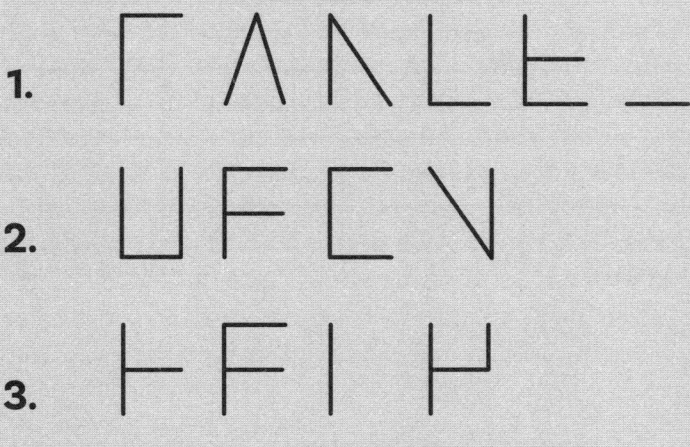

1.
2.
3.
4.

SCREEN SHOT

It is important during training to follow instructions. The screen below has four rows going across, 1, 2, 3 and 4, and four columns going down, A, B, C and D. Delete all the windows on the screen according to the instructions below. When you have finished, a space first will be revealed.

	A	B	C	D
1	DOG	SINGLE	IGLOO	BELLS
2	CREW	TANGLE	TEAM	TROUT
3	MONKEY	JINGLE	FOOD	CHEATER
4	EXTRA	TINGLE	SOLO	FOXES

1. Remove the windows that have two letter 'O's in column C.
2. Remove each window in column D that is an anagram of people who work in a school.
3. Remove the names of any animal that has travelled in space.
4. Remove any word that contains the Roman letter for TEN.
5. Remove the words in row 2 that are people who work together in a group.
6. Remove words in column B that start with a letter in the second half of the alphabet.

TESTING, TESTING

Training is nearly finished and the last thing to be done is to take a test. Join the astronauts and take the test below. Is there something rather unusual about the questions? You are quite right! Is someone trying to trick you? Yes they are!

1. There was a serious accident when a spacecraft crashed into a mountainside. Rescuers had to act quickly. Where did they bury the survivors?

2. Which word is always spelt incorrectly in the dictionary?

3. Satellite A is returning from space as satellite B is leaving Earth. The returning satellite is returning twice as fast as the one being launched. Which satellite is nearer to Earth when they meet? Is it A or B?

4. There are two astronauts in front of an astronaut, two astronauts behind an astronaut and one astronaut is in the middle. What is the least number of astronauts waiting to enter the simulation test area?

5. Which time of day appears the same whether it is spelt backwards or forwards? If you write it in capital letters, it reads the same if you look at it upside down!

CARL SAGAN

One of the most renowned names in popular science throughout the 20th century, Carl Sagan did much to bring scientific awareness into the mainstream, writing and talking extensively on everything from the search for alien life to environmental factors affecting our own planet.

Born in 1934 in New York City, Sagan showed a keen interest in nature and science, the latter encouraged in part by a love of science-fiction. He was a gifted student at school, fascinated by all science subjects, in particular astronomy, and would go on to enrol in university at the age of 16, where he earned Bachelor of Arts and Bachelor of Science degrees, followed by a Master's degree in science and a PhD in astronomy and astrophysics. The young Sagan also worked closely with famed astronomer Gerard Kuiper, after whom the Kuiper Belt at the edge of our Solar System is named.

Sagan would eventually begin working as an advisor to NASA, and played a role in many high-profile missions throughout the 1960s and 70s, from briefing the Apollo astronauts being sent to the Moon to the Mariner and Viking missions that went to Venus and Mars. He was also involved in programmes to send probes to the outer reaches of the Solar System; it was Sagan who designed the gold plaques attached to *Pioneer 10* and *11*, and the golden record attached to *Voyager 1* and *2*, which were intended to provide intelligent life with an insight into humankind and the origins of the space probes. Sagan would also theorise that Jupiter's moon Europa might possess oceans of subsurface water that could hold life, and that humanity could learn much from the greenhouse effect of the planet Venus to better understand and prevent environmental catastrophe on Earth.

Sagan would write a number of bestselling books in his lifetime, but it was the television series *Cosmos: A Personal Voyage* that really brought him into the public consciousness. Airing in 1980, the award-winning show covered numerous scientific topics across 13 episodes and became one of the most-watched television programmes in US public broadcasting history. Sagan would gain further acclaim for the science-fiction novel *Contact*, published in 1985, which was later adapted into a movie starring Jodie Foster.

One of Sagan's most enduring contributions to science was his association with SETI, the search for extra-terrestrial intelligence, and his role in founding The Planetary Society, which continues to inspire and educate in matters focusing on space exploration to this day.

4. LAUNCH DAY

It's finally launch day. The astronauts are fit and healthy, fully trained and ready to embark on their mission. Their spacecraft is safe and ready to go, fully stocked with space food and scientific equipment. The rocket, also known as the launch vehicle, which will propel the spacecraft out of Earth's gravitational pull, is fuelled, primed and waiting on the launch pad. Years of hard work have all led up to this moment.

Launch days are selected very carefully, taking a number of factors into consideration. Some of these are simple, such as weather conditions – clouds mean poor visibility, high winds interfere with flight and storms can damage equipment. But there are other, more complicated factors to consider, like the position of Earth with respect to its target. This is called orbital mechanics, and mission planners need to work out the best day for a launch based on the rotation of Earth, and the paths planets and asteroids take as they orbit the Sun. The period when things are calculated to line up just right is called the launch window, and this typically lasts a few weeks, while Earth is at the ideal point of its orbit around the Sun. The time of day is also considered, to take into account Earth's rotation and to make sure the launch site is facing the right direction in the Solar System. Once these conditions have been calculated, the launch date is booked in for a day with the ideal weather forecast within that window. But weather can be unpredictable and often launches are cancelled at the last minute, to be rescheduled for the next possible date in the launch window. About half of all last-minute cancellations are due to bad weather.

Once there's a day that ticks all the boxes, the launch can proceed. The day before the launch, the rocket is fuelled and powered up, and the spacecraft is readied. The spacecraft the astronauts will travel in is located at the very top of the rocket, so they get on board by taking a lift to the top of the 'service structure'. This is a steel framework built on the launch pad that stands next to the rocket, allowing for access at every level for entry, safety checks and maintenance. Once inside, the astronauts are fastened into their seats, which are tilted on their backs. Not only does this mean they're facing the direction of travel (up!), but it also means they can withstand the G-force of lift off without losing consciousness. Sitting upright, their blood would rush to their feet, causing them to pass out. Five or ten minutes before launch, the countdown begins. The crew and astronauts have done all the final preparations, so now it's over to the launch software to finish the sequence. If it detects an error, it could still safely abort the launch, but if all goes smoothly, we have lift off!

The rocket's engines generate a huge amount of force to lift it off the ground and travel fast enough to escape Earth's gravity. Most rockets are made up of multiple segments, called stages. Each stage has its own engines, and once their fuel is used up, the stage drops away as the rocket climbs. When one stage drops away, the next set of engines ignite, propelling the now lighter rocket up through the atmosphere. When the final stage burns out, the spacecraft separates, and the next leg of its journey begins: into space.

COUNTDOWN

The countdown is about to begin!

Here's a quick counting puzzle to tackle.

A triangle is a shape with three sides.

How many triangles appear in the picture?

HINT: As well as counting the small individual triangles, you can combine triangles together to form larger triangles. You can also combine a triangle with any other shape to form larger triangles.

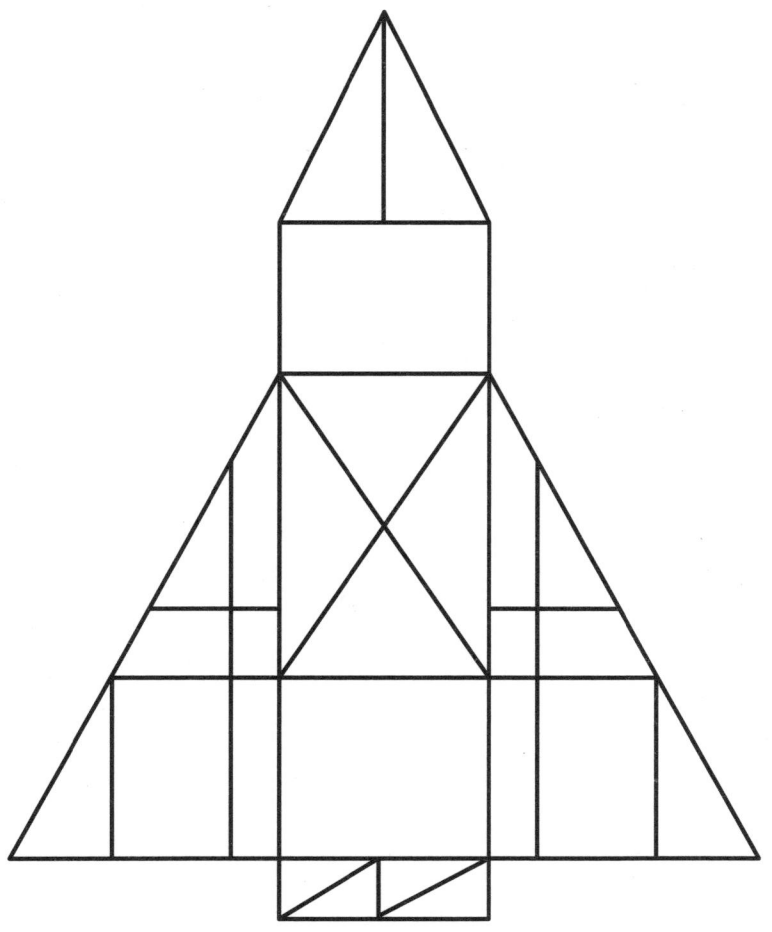

TEN □ □ □

The countdown begins. Solve the TEN clues below.
Each answer contains the word TEN.

1. Happy, not worried   _ _ _ T E N _

2. Tries to hear something   _ _ _ T E N _

3. Happening a lot, frequently   _ _ T E N

4. Make something longer   _ _ T E N _

5. An aerial   _ _ T E N _ _

6. Do something which is not for real, such as acting in a play

                                                            _ _ _ T E N _

7. A tool, usually in a kitchen   _ T E N _ _ _

8. This starts with a capital letter and finishes with a full stop

                                                            _ _ _ T E N _ _

9. Place to sleep under canvas   T E N _

10. It attaches a muscle to a bone   T E N _ _ _

NINE . . .

Nine numbered boxes. Nine different letters of the alphabet. Solve the clues and write the letters in the appropriate spaces in the grid. When all nine letters are in place, the name of a Space Shuttle will be revealed.

1	2	3	4	5	6	7	8	9

CLUES

1. Describes space food with all the moisture taken out.

   1 8 2 7 1

2. Weather that has sub-zero temperatures, and a white surface.

   2 4 9

3. Part of a helmet that covers the face, which you can see through.

   6 2 3 5 8

EIGHT . . .

On launch day, everything has to go according to plan, in fact it has to go like clockwork! In this puzzle each answer has a total of eight letters. Write the answer words in the grid, with each first letter going in a numbered square. Then you have to decide whether to write the answer in a clockwise or anticlockwise direction. All the answers have to interlock together. The first answer begins with 'U'.

1. The whole cosmos.

2. A skilled mechanic, the person who builds technical equipment.

3. Each 24 hours, all the time (2 words, 5 letters and 3 letters).

4. A very famous scientist called Albert.

5. A small rocky object, that orbits the Sun.

6. The opposite of take-offs.

7. Periods of travel from one place to another.

8. Chosen, picked out, such as when an astronaut is chosen for training.

SEVEN . . .

The listed words all contain seven letters. Fit them back in the frame to read either across or down. One letter is keyed in. Take care! There is only one way to get all the words to fit back in place.

AIRLOCK   INSTALL   ROCKETS

ATTEMPT   JUPITER   SPUTNIK

CLOSING   MISSION   SURFACE

DRAWING   NEPTUNE   TRANSIT

SIX . . .

All answers have six letters and fit into the grid reading in a clockwise direction. The second letter of Clue 1 is R, as shown. After that you have to work out in which hexagonal cell the answer begins.

CLUES

1. Make a journey.
2. Very intelligent, knowing a lot.
3. Make something from scratch.
4. The many segments rockets are made up of.
5. Noises, things you hear.
6. One sixtieth of an hour.
7. Easy, not complicated.
8. An item of headgear that protects your head.
9. Shiny, glowing, not dull or dark.
10. A pilot or aviator.
11. Planet visited by *Voyager 2*.
12. This country worked with Western countries on the International Space Station.

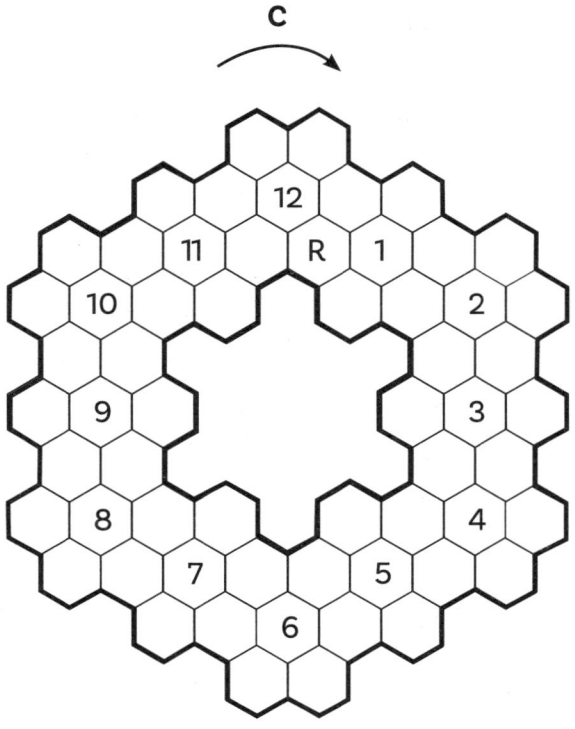

FIVE . . .

A word square reads the same whether you look across or down. There are FIVE words reading ACROSS and the same FIVE words reading DOWN, which all interlock. We give you FOUR words to make up a 5 x 5 word square. Clearly, there is a word missing. It's the name of a planet. Can you work out what it is and complete the word square?

AWARE

HERDS

RARER

TREAD

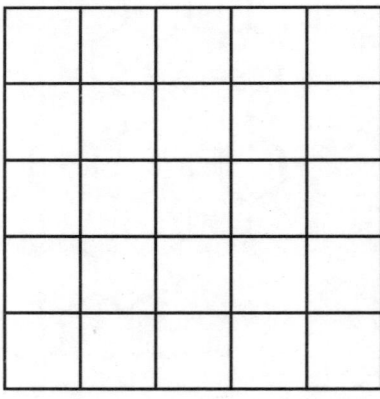

FOUR . . .

The weather is a very important part of launch day. If it is bad, launch day cannot go ahead.

In the following sentences you will find a weather warning that may delay a take-off.

The weather words can be found by joining together words and parts of words. They will always be found as a line of letters. All weather words are FOUR letters long.

1. There is no way we can launch today.

2. I grow in doubt about the timing of take-off.

3. Against launching them is the terrible weather.

4. Heavy storms could drag us to a different place.

5. I beg a leaving date is put back.

HINT: Here are some weather hazard words.

GALE GUST MIST SNOW WIND

THREE . . .

There are THREE letters of the alphabet that do NOT appear in the box of letters. Work out the missing letters then use them to name something that is a vital part of our Solar System.

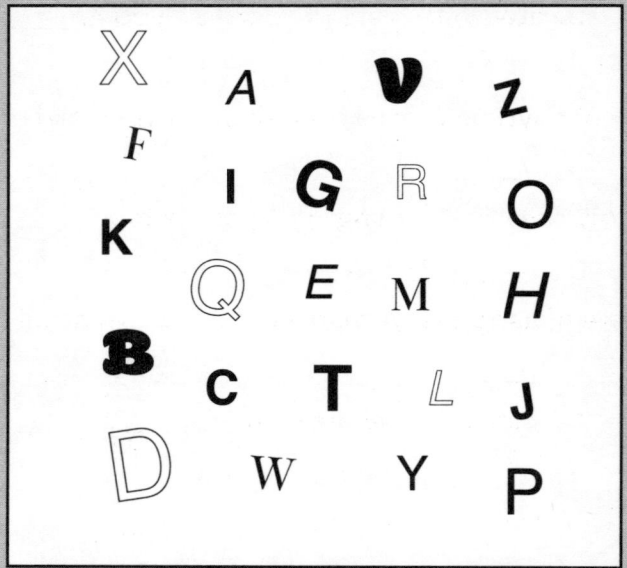

TWO...

The countdown is almost over. We're nearly there. This puzzle is about pairs of meanings. Some words sound the same but have two different meanings. In fact pair, sounds exactly the same as pear, pair means two items and pear is a fruit.

1. Listen to / In this place _____ / _____

2. Colour associated with Mars / Looked at a book _____ / _____

3. The light of daytime comes from this / A male child of parents _____ / _____

4. Check how heavy something is / A path or road _____ / _____

5. First name of astronaut Armstrong / Get down on all fours _____ / _____

6. Groups of 60 minutes / Belonging to us _____ / _____

7. An aircraft / Ordinary, not fancy _____ / _____

8. Steps, to a capsule for example, / Look for a long time _____ / _____

ONE...

The countdown is almost over. We are down to ONE. In the sentences below, the word ONE appears many times. It can appear inside another word, or it can link one word to another. How many times? Clue: more than ONE, but fewer than TEN!

Galileo never could have imagined the impact of his telescope. Isaac Newton, early scientist, made discoveries that are still used today.

Planets and dwarf planets have been discovered down the ages, Pluto, Neptune to name but two.

Putting a man on the Moon eventually happened in 1969, sooner than some people thought. US President Nixon phoned the astronauts to say, 'Well done!'

On a space mission everyone must work together. The International Space Station even has astronauts from different nations working together.

LIFT OFF!

The pictures may look alike. Look again! There are FIVE differences between picture A and picture B. Try to spot the lot.

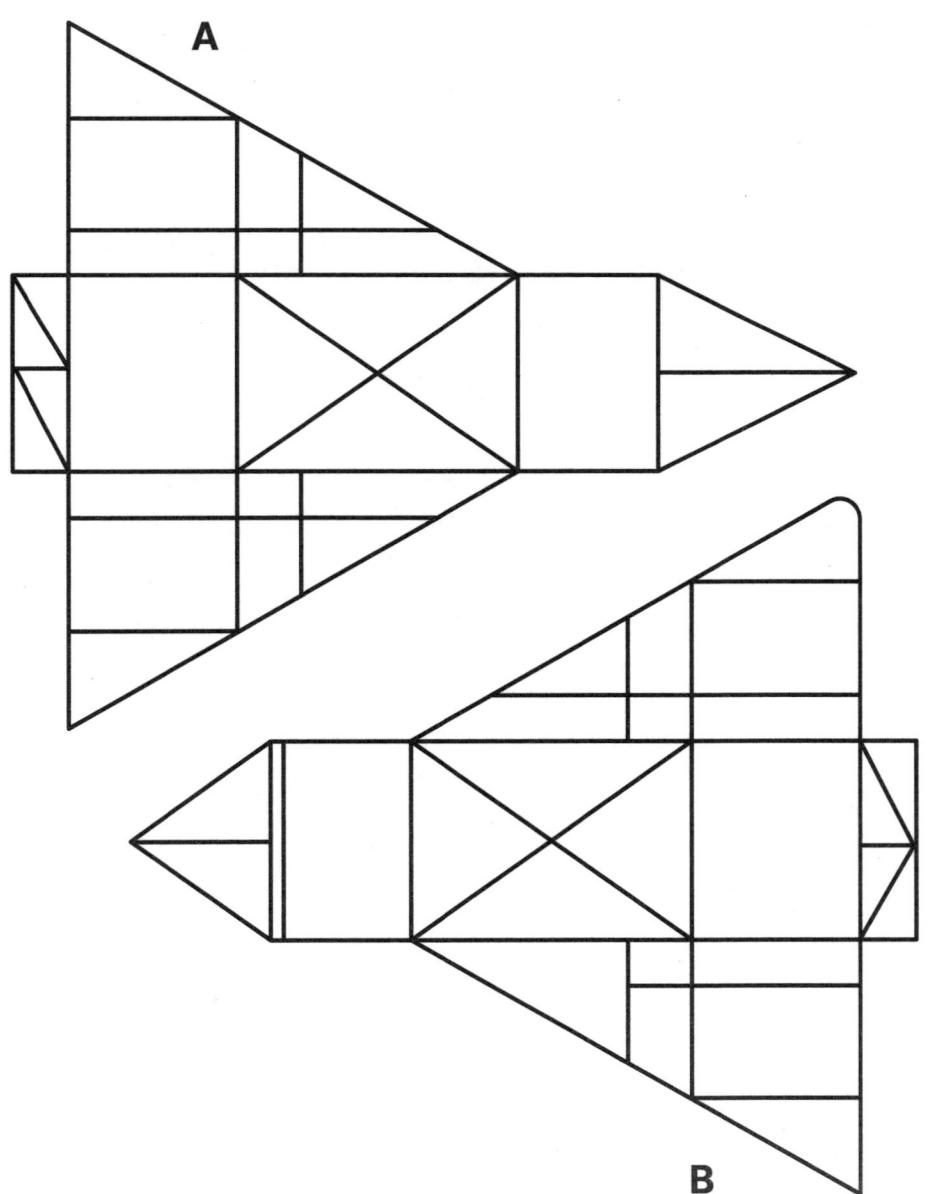

VALENTINA TERESHKOVA

The Space Race of the 1950s and 60s saw the Soviet Union score several notables firsts: the first satellite in space, the first animal in space, the first man in space – and in 1963 it achieved another victory over its American rivals when Valentina Tereshkova was launched into orbit, in the process becoming the first woman in space.

Born in 1937 in a village northeast of Moscow, Tereshkova developed a passion for parachuting and made her first jump in 1959 aged 22. This led to her training as a competitive skydiver – a decision that would ultimately prove instrumental to young Tereshkova being recruited into the Soviet Union's space programme. Following a selection process that started with approximately 400 candidates, Tereshkova was eventually picked alongside four other women to begin cosmonaut training. While they would endure a programme much like that of their male counterparts, unlike the men, neither Tereshkova nor her fellow trainees came from a military background; she was subsequently made a lieutenant in the Soviet Air Force.

Tereshkova would launch into space on 16 June 1963 aboard *Vostok 6* and remain in orbit of Earth for almost three days, during which time she orbited the planet a total of 48 times. She would spend much of her time conducting scientific experiments devoted to investigating the effects of space travel on human beings, but she nevertheless still made time to enjoy the view: looking down from her space capsule, she would remark 'how beautiful Earth is'.

The Vostok 6 mission would make Tereshkova not only the first woman in space, but also the only woman to fly a solo mission in space. Incredibly, over 60 years later she still holds this record.

Much like her male counterpart Yuri Gagarin, Tereshkova's mission made her something of a celebrity. She travelled the world continuously in the years after her mission, often hailed as a feminist icon and role model – proof in a male-dominated era that women were every bit as capable as men.

Although Tereshkova was keen to travel to space again, her Vostok mission would remain the only time she would ever find herself in orbit. She nevertheless continued to play a role in the Soviet space programme as an instructor at Star City near Moscow, and would earn a doctorate in aeronautical engineering. Outside of the space programme, she would become politically active, a career she pursued with even greater interest after retiring from the Air Force.

5. LIVING IN SPACE

On an average mission, astronauts will spend about six months in space. That's six months of eating, sleeping, working and exercising in a strange environment our bodies weren't built for. Understanding the effects of living in space is key for keeping astronauts physically and mentally healthy throughout their mission and for when they return to Earth. Scientists and engineers have had to develop various ways of adapting spacecraft to either simulate features of Earth's environment or meet the body's needs in a different way.

The first requirement is the most basic: breathing. Space is a vacuum, meaning it contains no matter or gas whatsoever. Spacecraft life support systems therefore have to provide breathable air, processing it to remove the carbon dioxide we breathe out and to replace the oxygen we need to breathe in, much like trees do on Earth. The spacecraft itself must be completely airtight, otherwise this precious gas would be sucked out into space – it is a completely closed system that continuously recycles the air.

Along with fresh air, drinkable water is crucial to staying alive. Tanks of fresh water are loaded into the spacecraft for launch, but for longer missions, the amount of water needed would be too heavy to transport. The air recycling systems also salvage water vapour from the astronauts' sweat and breath to turn it back into clean drinking water. On the International Space Station, up to 80 per cent of the water astronauts drink has actually been recycled in this way, in its own mini water cycle.

Space food is probably the most famous aspect of life in space. It has to be nutritious to keep astronauts healthy but must be preserved to last for long journeys, whether it's in tins and tubes or freeze-dried. Early space food mainly consisted of dry cubes, powders and pastes made of real foods like meat and fruits, but astronauts didn't find them very appetising. Although they gave the astronauts the nourishment they needed, enjoying food is really important from a psychological perspective, too. Nowadays, space food tries to replicate the experience of eating meals like chicken salad, cheese and crackers, or even steak. Astronauts must be mindful of crumbs, though, as it's hard to clean up when they're floating all around the cabin!

The weightlessness of space, called microgravity, has strange effects on the human body. Most immediately, it affects astronauts' balance and coordination, and much like sailors getting their 'sea legs', their brains have to adapt to this new feeling and there being no up or down. Prolonged time spent under microgravity causes the muscles, bones and heart to become weaker, because they aren't working against gravity any more. To combat this, astronauts have to exercise even more than they do on Earth, typically around two hours a day. This exercise also has to be adapted for space – treadmills and exercise bikes have harnesses and straps that pull the user down on to them to mimic the effect of gravity, and a special weights machine uses vacuum cylinders to add resistance to a bar that users can lift or squat with.

Research is still being done on the effects of space travel on the body, such as how the absence of day and night affects our internal body clock. Animals and plants are also being flown into space to see if seeds will grow and eggs will hatch, exploring the possibilities of growing fresh food off-Earth. As we start to plan for longer missions, to Mars and even beyond, our ways of supporting life in space will develop and grow too.

QUOTE

Solve the clues and write your answers reading across in the upper grid. When you have completed this grid, transfer the key-coded letters to the lower grid. The first letter you need is in B6, so slide your finger from column B down to row 6 and you will find the letter F. Write this in the lower grid. When this lower grid is complete you will be able to complete a quotation that begins, 'Popping outside...' It was said by a famous astronaut who spent some time living in space. Column A reading down will give you his name.

CLUES

1. Implements or devices to help you do a job.
2. Picture, likeness.
3. An award made up of a metal circle and ribbon given for a major achievement.
4. Strength, force that makes a spacecraft work.
5. Our planet.
6. The opposite of before.
7. Has information.
8. Go into.

	A	B	C	D	E
1					
2					
3					
4					
5					
6		F			
7					
8					

B6	B1	E4		B5	A1	D7	C2	E3	A7	
F										

C8	C1	B2	B4	C5	E8	C7	C4	

RECYCLING

Recycling is difficult in space. The main thing that is recycled is water, including water produced from sweat and urine.

The names of items that can be recycled on Earth are listed below. Their letters have been mixed up in alphabetical order. Can you recycle the letters and make new words? We give you a clue.

1. A G L S S _____ (see-through material)

2. A E P P R _____ (used for writing on)

3. C E H L O S T _____ (wear these)

4. E E E L N O P S V _____ (put stamps in the corner of them)

5. A A B C D D O R R _____ (thick type of answer 2)

6. A C I L P S T _____ (used to make boxes and containers)

7. A B E E I R S T T _____ (they power torches and phones)

8. A B E E L O R S T T T W _____/_____ (two words – they provide liquid to refresh)

STICK TOGETHER

In space, items must be anchored or stuck together to prevent them from floating off. Look at the two lists of words. Can you stick two words together to make a new word? Each word is used once, and every word should be used.

1. AIR   PAD

2. CAR   SUIT

3. COUNT   LIGHT

4. LAUNCH   GO

5. MEAL   LOCK

6. MOON   RISE

7. SPACE   DOWN

8. SUN   TIMES

KEEPING FIT

Regular exercise is an important part of an astronaut's daily routine. All types of exercise can take place during a space mission – under special conditions, of course. Major Tim Peake even managed a marathon in space, only the second astronaut to do so.

Look at the words linked to keeping fit. Search for the words in the box of letters. These words can go in any direction, forwards, backwards, up, down or diagonally. One word in the list has floated off into space and you will not be able to find it in the grid. What is it?

BENDS

BICEP CURLS

BIKE

BODY

CYCLE

EXERCISE

FITNESS

GYM

HEART

JOG

LIFT

MACHINES

MARATHON

MUSCLES

PEDAL

RUN

SPORT

SQUATS

STEPS

STRETCH

TREADMILL

WALK

WEIGHTS

B	B	O	T	X	S	J	U	L	E	Y	T
R	I	J	R	T	E	W	A	L	K	V	R
W	K	C	A	M	O	D	C	I	M	R	E
H	E	U	E	L	E	Y	B	F	A	L	A
S	Q	I	H	P	C	R	E	T	C	Z	D
S	W	R	G	Y	C	S	W	G	H	S	M
E	P	B	D	H	I	U	O	P	I	P	I
N	E	O	E	C	T	J	R	U	N	E	L
T	B	U	R	N	G	S	K	L	E	T	L
I	R	E	J	T	D	I	O	H	S	S	W
F	X	S	E	L	C	S	U	M	Y	G	E
E	N	D	M	A	R	A	T	H	O	N	Y

THE BRUSH-OFF

Everyday tasks like cleaning your teeth can be a real challenge in space. Water can rise up and the toothbrush and the paste could float away!

Here are seven toothbrushes that have all been fixed together to keep them in one place.

Taking the top toothbrush off the pile each time, in which order would you pick them up?

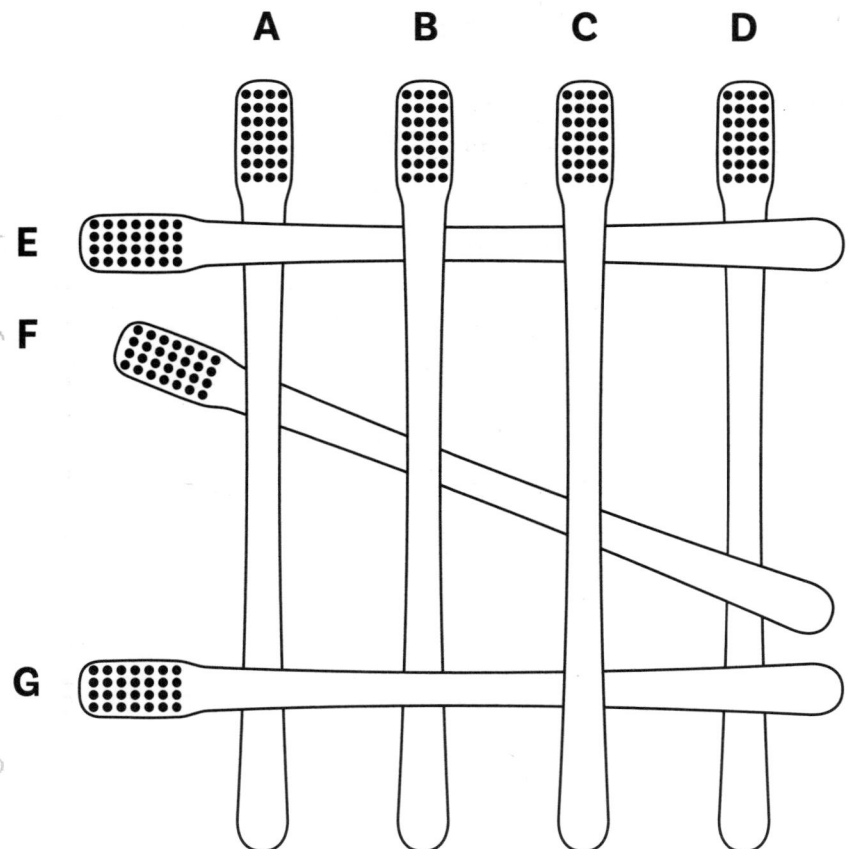

FABULOUS FOOD

The names of different space food favourites are represented by different symbols. The first group of symbols stands for CHICKEN. The symbols remain the same throughout, e.g. If C is a white circle in the first group, C is a white circle in all the groups. Can you work your way through the menu and identify the different foods?

KEEP IT TIDY

In a spacecraft, every available inch of space has to be used.

Here's a rack of shelving where boxes of items are stored. One of the astronauts has the task of sorting out three of the boxes to make sure things are properly packed away and to get rid of anything that is no longer needed. He made a note of the THREE boxes he was to look out for but let go of the piece of paper and it floated away! The astronaut is certain that two boxes were side by side on the same row. All three boxes had different letters to identify them.

The checking list, which is, fortunately, attached to the wall, gives the most recent boxes that have been sorted.

All the boxes on the bottom row were sorted yesterday.

Three other boxes in column B were sorted the day before.

The odd-numbered boxes marked with an A along with C2 and D1 were checked last week.

Which three boxes does our astronaut have to check?

	A	B	C	D
1				
2				
3				
4				

GUION BLUFORD

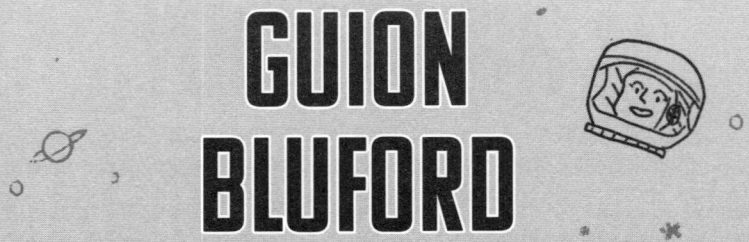

In the 1960s, a test pilot named Robert Lawrence was selected to be the United States' first African American astronaut. Lawrence's untimely death during a test flight in 1967 meant that he never got to fulfil his dream of going to space, and it would be another 16 years before an African-American named Guion Bluford would achieve that goal.

Bluford was born in 1942 and studied engineering at university, receiving a Bachelor of Science degree in aerospace engineering in 1964. After graduating from university, Bluford joined the United States Air Force, and would later go on to work as an instructor pilot from the late 1960s to the early 1970s. In 1974, he would receive a Master of Science degree in aerospace engineering from the Air Force Institute of Technology and then go on to work at the Air Force Flight Dynamics Laboratory, first as deputy for advanced concepts at the Aeromechanics division before becoming chief at the Aerodynamics and Airframe branch.

In 1978, however, Bluford's life would change forever. NASA had recruited Nichelle Nichols – famed for playing Lt. Uhura on the science-fiction television series *Star Trek* – to help encourage applications from women and people from minority communities to apply for the astronaut programme. Bluford was one of those applicants, becoming part of NASA astronaut Group 8, and after a year of training he officially became an astronaut in August 1979.

It would be four years until he was actually assigned to a mission, but when the Space Shuttle *Challenger* launched from the Kennedy Space Centre on 30 August 1983 for mission STS-8, Bluford officially became the first African American in space.

Two years later, Bluford would travel into space for the second time, once again aboard the *Challenger*, for mission STS-61-A. This mission was unique for carrying eight astronauts into space, which remains the largest crew to ever take part in one mission. Sadly, it was also the final time the *Challenger* flew before its tragic loss in early 1986.

Bluford would be assigned to two further Space Shuttle missions – STS-39 in 1991 and STS-53 in 1992 – both aboard the *Discovery*. He would retire from NASA in 1993 after spending a total of 688 hours in space across his four shuttle missions.

ROCKETMAN

There are NINE different letters of the alphabet in the word ROCKETMAN.

In the grid, every row and every column must contain the letters in ROCKETMAN but not in this order. Each 3 x 3 box must contain the letters in ROCKETMAN as well.

Look at the centre box. It contains the letters OCKETMAN, so the empty box must contain the letter R. Look across at the third row down. The blank spaces must contain R and E as all the other letters in ROCKETMAN are in place. The E can't go in the first blank space as there is already an E in that 3 x 3 square, so it must be the R. The E goes in the other blank space on that row. Now, over to you to complete the grid.

E		N	R		O	C		A
C	O		N	A	T		M	K
		O	T	M	E	K		
N			K		C			T
		M	O	N	A	R		
A	K		M	E	N		C	R
M		C	A		K	T		E

WATCH IT!

Although conditions are very different when living in space, time can still be measured.

Can you measure up to this time teaser?

Draw one straight line across the watch that divides the face into two sections.

Each section must contain six numbers.

Add one group of six numbers together. Then add the other six numbers together. The totals MUST be the same.

Where would the line need to be drawn?

CUBE FOOD

In the early years of space travel, food was made into bite-sized cubes or powdered and was not very appetising. Things have changed in recent years, and in 2001 a pizza party actually took place on the International Space Station.

In this puzzle you must complete the cubes with the words listed. When completed, the words in each cube will read the same across and down. Each cube contains the word CUBE!

BOLD	DESK	ICED
CUBE	EBBS	ITCH
CUBE	ENDS	TRUE
CUBE	HEEL	UPON

SPACE FACTS

The Saturn V rockets used for the Apollo missions took about 12 seconds to clear the launch tower after the ignition of their engines.

Saturn V rockets stood 111 metres high – taller than the Statue of Liberty!

Saturn V rockets were made mainly of aluminium but also used several other materials, including titanium and polyurethane – and even cork!

MICROGRAVITY

Objects in an area of microgravity seem weightless, almost like they are in free fall. Everything from a sleeping bag to a toothbrush has to be fixed to stop it floating away.

Solve the clues in this puzzle. The answer words might be floating. Float up and you will read one word. Float down and you will read another, which is the first word backwards.

down

1. Goes round and round.

   Cuts, usually with scissors.

up

down

2. Leather strip, that holds things in place in a spacecraft.

   Small items that are important in machines.

up

3. A former space station.
   Outer edge of a wheel.

down

up

4. Vapour, air.
   Sink, droop.

down

up

5. It twinkles in the sky at night.
   Rodents that have travelled
   in space.

down

up

SALLY RIDE

One of the Soviet Union's early victories in the Space Race occurred in 1963 when Valentina Tereshkova became the first woman in space. Remarkably, it would take the United States 20 years to match this achievement – but the woman who made the historic flight would become a significant figure in America's space travel story.

Sally Ride was born in 1951 in Los Angeles. As a young woman she considered pursuing a career as a professional tennis player before deciding to focus on her academic studies, going on to earn degrees in physics and English, and later a Master's degree and PhD in physics.

Ride's life would change forever in early 1977, however, when she responded to a NASA recruitment programme. From around 8,000 applicants, she was eventually selected to be one of just 35 people who made up NASA Astronaut Group 8, and one of just six women to be included. In the years that followed, Ride would work as ground-based support for NASA missions and help develop the Remote Manipulator System – or robot arm – that would be used on many Space Shuttle missions. Eventually, in April 1982, she was announced as the first American woman to be assigned to a shuttle mission.

Ride would fly into space twice, in 1983 as part of STS-7, and then again in 1984 as part of STS-41-G, both missions aboard the Space Shuttle *Challenger*. She would spend a total of just over 14 days in orbit across her two spaceflights, and her skills as a mission specialist – from conducting scientific experiments to manipulating the shuttle's robot arm in precision operations – would prove invaluable.

Challenger was tragically lost during a launch in January 1986, and Ride's considerable experience with, and knowledge of, the shuttle meant that she would play a key role in the investigation to determine the cause of the disaster, as well as in 2003 when the Space Shuttle *Columbia* was also lost. While she would leave NASA in 1987, space would continue to play a huge role in Sally Ride's life: in senior roles at prestigious US universities, as director of the California Space Institute and a member of the President's Committee of Advisors on Science and Technology. She would also co-author books and start her own company, Sally Ride Science, dedicated to educating and inspiring youngsters to engage in science.

Sally Ride died in 2012. For all the incredible 'firsts' of her life – the first American woman in space, the first woman to serve as the capsule communicator at mission control, and the first member of the LGBTQ+ community to have flown in space – it is perhaps her work inspiring the next generation that has most assured her place in space history.

THE FINAL STRAW

Straws come in handy when you need to have a drink out in space.

Here's a sum made up of numbers made out of straws. 1 + 1 = 11. That can't be right!

By moving just one straw, can you make a different sum to which the answer is 130?

Sounds tricky? This is a bit of a trick. It's the final straw!

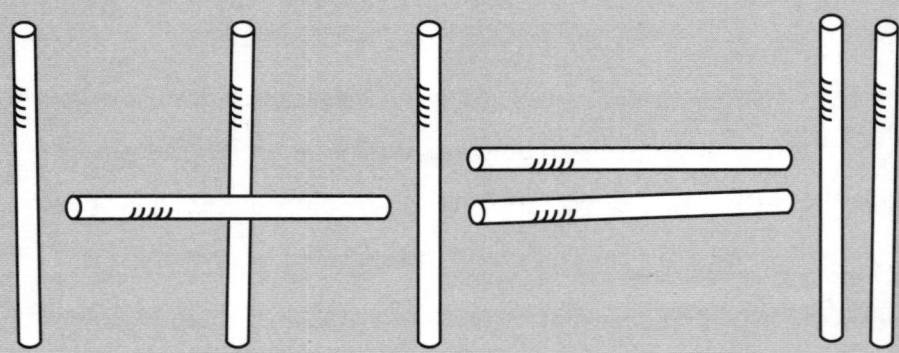

SPACE FACTS

Incredibly, the smartphone in your pocket has more computing power than not only the Apollo Guidance Computer that was used to send astronauts to the Moon, but also more power than all the computers that were in use at NASA in 1969!

Rockets can be propelled by liquid fuels, solid fuels or a combination of both.

Solid rocket fuels are made up of a combination of organic matter or powdered aluminium and an oxidiser such as ammonium perchlorate. Once they are ignited, solid fuels burn until they run out.

6. SCIENCE IN SPACE

Not only are astronauts explorers, they're also fully trained scientists! Scientific experiments are an important part of many missions, especially those on space stations, which are big, habitable spacecraft used as long-term bases for space crews to live and work on. The most important one is the International Space Station (ISS), a collaborative mission involving five space agencies and 15 countries worldwide. Since its launch in 1998, over 3,000 experiments have been conducted on board the ISS, from measuring deep space radiation to growing tomatoes.

In order to fully explore and understand space, lots of different instruments and equipment are used. Telescopes allow us to see space in different types of light, such as the visible light our eyes can see, but also invisible light like ultraviolet and infrared. This light doesn't just let us see the wonders of the universe, it can actually be analysed to tell us what different stars, planets and nebulae (clouds of dust and gas) are made from, what temperature they are and whether they have an atmosphere like Earth. Radiation detection is also crucial: exposure to too much radiation in space can have long-term health effects on astronauts or future space colonists, but if we know what type of radiation is out there and how strong it is, we can work out where it's safest to go and protect ourselves with special suits and radiation shields.

Experiments also help us to develop technology for future space missions. Different materials are tested to see how they behave in space. In 2019, astronauts mixed cement on the ISS, which is a microgravity environment. Microgravity describes when the gravitational force acting on objects is very weak, and the objects appear to be weightless. They discovered that cement actually forms in a different way in this environment, which helps us to understand how it might be used to build settlements off-world, such as lunar bases. As well as testing materials, scientists explore new life support systems, such as ways of recycling urine into drinking water, and even how to farm in space. Astronauts have managed to hatch quails and grow lettuce and tomatoes, as farming food off-Earth will be key to long-distance missions and maybe even living on other planets.

But these experiments don't just teach us about space or how we might eventually live there, they can tell us about life on Earth, too. Seeds and beans send their roots down and their shoots up when they're on Earth, but would they still manage this without gravity and the Sun to guide them? (The answer is: the leaves grow towards the light source but the roots grow in all directions!)

And just as there are telescopes and instruments in space for gathering information on other planets and distant galaxies, there are those designed to look back at our own planet. This is called Earth observation, and while it's largely conducted by uncrewed satellites, astronauts do their fair share too. Earth observation is very useful for monitoring the environment: it can track oil spills, measure the health of rainforests, monitor sea ice levels and help predict natural disasters such as floods and wildfires.

DATA TRANSFER

In any type of experiment it is important to back up all data.
Follow the lines and copy the letters into the empty circles, so
that all info is safely stored.

The message tells you the outcome of your work.

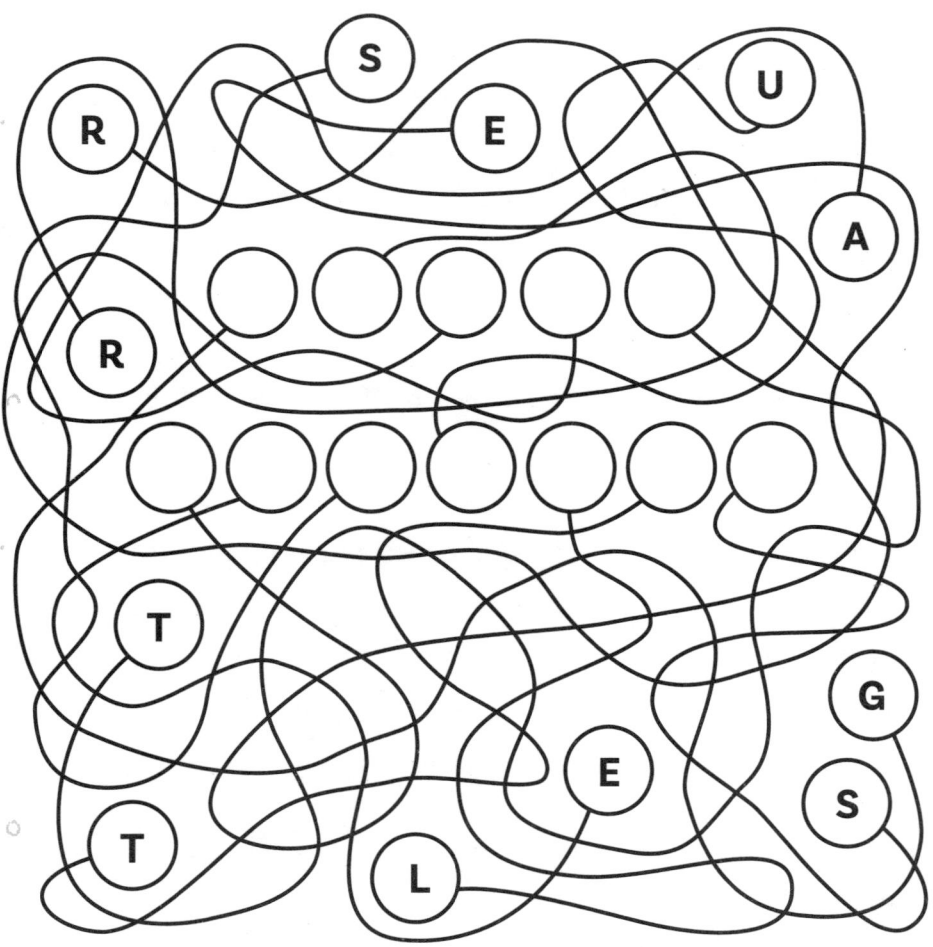

LAIKA

It might surprise you to learn that the first living beings to venture into space weren't in fact humans, and instead of astronauts it was animals who would be strapped into rockets and be the first to see our planet from orbit.

Monkeys, dogs and mice were commonly used by both the United States and Soviet Russia during the Space Race of the early 1950s and 60s, and a dog called Laika is perhaps the most well-known of these. While she wasn't actually the first living creature in space, this plucky little pooch was the first to make a complete orbit of our planet, assuring her of a place in the history of space travel.

Aged approximately three years old, Laika was a stray mongrel found wandering the streets of Moscow. Just like the human astronauts that would follow in her footsteps, Laika was put through a series of tests to prepare her for her mission; these included keeping her in small cages for extended periods of time to simulate the confined conditions of the capsule destined to carry her into orbit, and placing her in a centrifuge to acclimatise her to the extreme pressures of a rocket launch.

Laika was launched into space aboard *Sputnik* 2 on 3 November 1957. Sadly, this intrepid mission was to be her only voyage – her life signs faced during her fourth orbit of Earth. Her sacrifice nevertheless played an important role in our understanding of space travel – as well as promoting discussion as to the ethics of using animals for scientific experimentation – and paved the way for humans to venture safely into space in the years that followed. As a result, Laika will forever be remembered as a pivotal figure in the story of humanity's quest for the stars.

SPACE FACTS

The final mission of the Apollo space programme was Apollo 17, which travelled to the Moon in December 1972. This was the longest lunar mission, lasting over 12 days!

During the Apollo 17 mission, astronauts travelled an incredible 4.7 miles (7.6 kilometres) from their landing site using the Lunar Roving Vehicle.

Lunar Roving Vehicles, or moon buggies as they were called, were transported to the Moon for Apollos 15, 16 and 17. These four-wheeled vehicles allowed astronauts to travel further away from their lunar modules than earlier missions, as well as allowing them to carry heavy equipment for scientific experiments. All three LRVs are still on the Moon's surface today!

ORBITS

Scientific experiments in space are based on observation and calculating using the evidence that you have recorded. As you orbit round the planets you will come across a series of numbers. In each case there is a pattern established by the numbers given. Your mission is to fill in the blank section by deciding what is next to complete the orbit.

A to D are based purely on how the numbers relate to each other. E is slightly different, but we don't want to spell out the solution to you! (Yes, this IS a clue to finding the missing number!)

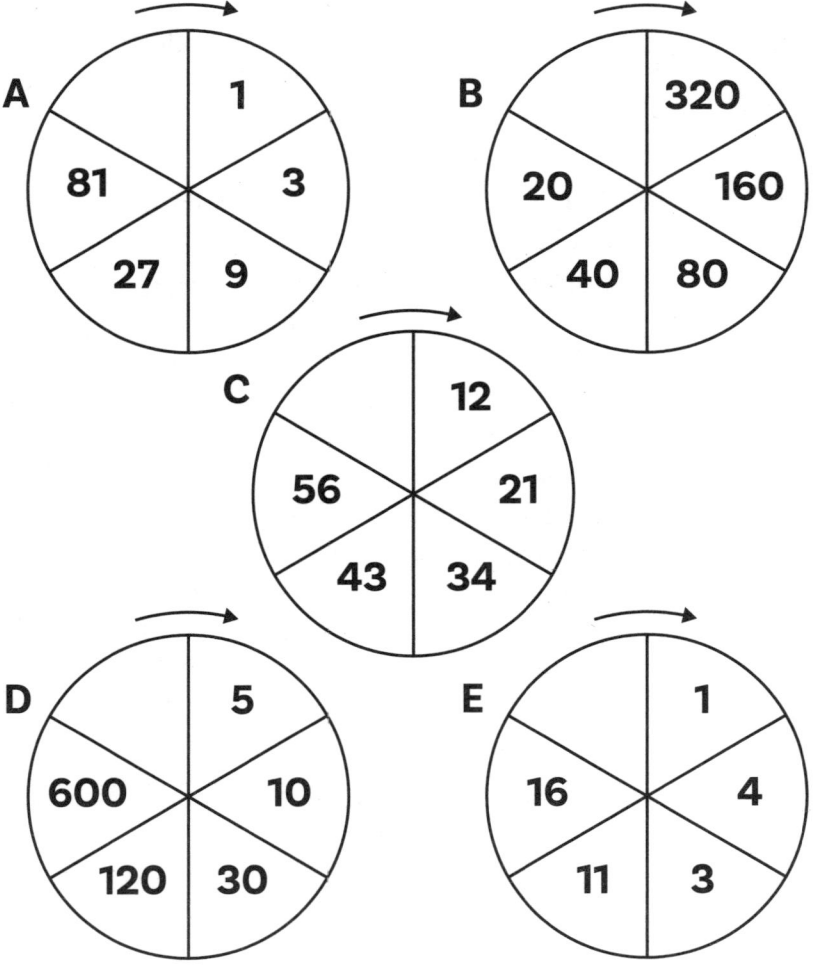

MAE JEMISON

Mae Jemison has enjoyed a diverse career across her adult life: from working as a doctor in Thailand, to serving in the Peace Corps, and training as an engineer; from starting her own technology research company and educational foundation that runs science-focused summer camps for teenagers, to writing books and appearing as a public speaker, where she uses her platform to inspire others to pursue STEM opportunities. Incredibly, somewhere in between all these roles she found the time to become the first African American woman to launch into space.

Born in 1956, Jemison's interest in space began in the 1960s as she developed an interest in science – not only from looking to the stars and following developments in the Space Race between the United States and Soviet Russia, but also by paying close attention to nature and the world around her. Fuelling her imagination further, the young Mae was inspired by the television series *Star Trek*, in particular the character of Lt. Uhura played by African American actress Nichelle Nichols.

Later inspiration came in the form of Sally Ride (the first American woman in space) and Guion Bluford (the first African American in space), and in 1987 Jemison was successful in applying for NASA's astronaut programme. Several years of training and launch support work followed before Jemison was selected to fly on STS-47 aboard the Space Shuttle *Endeavour*. Launched on 12 September 1992, Jemison's role aboard the shuttle was as mission specialist, with responsibility for conducting a number of scientific experiments across the almost eight days she spent in orbit.

A year after her shuttle mission, Jemison's life came full circle when in 1993 she was given the opportunity to appear on the very television show that had inspired her as a young girl, with a guest role in an episode of *Star Trek: The Next Generation* called 'Second Chances'.

Whether travelling aboard the real Space Shuttle *Endeavour* or the fictional USS *Enterprise*, Mae Jemison's life is every bit as inspiring as those of the role models she looked up to as a child. Once quoted as saying: "never limit yourself because of others' limited imaginations; never limit others because of your own limited imagination", she has helped pave the way for a new generation to follow in her footsteps and pursue their own dreams.

PLANT POWER

A new plant has been developed and grown in a spacecraft. The scientists calculate that it will have an incredible rate of growth. It is estimated that it will double in area in every 24 hours.

It started off in a 9cm container, known as a 'pillow'. It has already been moved into a larger container on three occasions. The present container is 1 metre square.

Calculations suggest that in two weeks, or 14 days' time, the super plant will fill its container.

On what day would the container be half-filled by the plant?

STEPS

Carrying out experiments in space can be a series of small steps. We give you the answer to the first clue in this puzzle. The answer to the second clue will be almost the same as the first but an additional letter will be added. You can change the order of the letters. Continue like this, adding letters until you have answered clue 5. Now you have to take a letter away each time until you come back to a word of three letters.

1. Earth's atmosphere.

2. Two matching items, such as gloves or shoes.

3. France has one of the oldest space programmes. What is France's capital city?

4. Tell someone how good they are, show admiration.

5. Celebrations, get-togethers.

6. One of 13 bands on the American flag, which was seen on the Moon in 1969.

7. Short journeys.

8. The edges of the fingers.

9. Get into position in a seat on take-off.

1	A	I	R				
2							
3							
4							
5							
6							
7							
8							
9							

MOVING ROBOTS

Two humanoid robots are being put through their paces. They respond to spoken commands, but their options are very limited.

At the command of LEFT the robot will move round 90 degrees to the left.

At the command of RIGHT the robot will move round 90 degrees to the right.

At the command of ABOUT TURN the robot will move round 180 degrees, so that it is now facing the opposite direction from its starting position.

The following commands are given:

LEFT

RIGHT

RIGHT

LEFT

RIGHT

ABOUT TURN

Robot A has a malfunction and does not move after carrying out the first order.

Robot B makes all the correct moves.

The two robots were both facing the same direction before the commands were given.

Are the robots facing the same direction after the movements?

FACE FACTS

When carrying out experiments in space, scientists look at the effect of space on the human body. In this puzzle, we are looking at different parts of the face. Letters have been replaced by symbols. The first answer is NOSE. Can you face facts and work out the other parts of the human face?

1. ☆ ☆ ✳ ✜

2. ✜ ✷ ✜ ✳

3. ✜ ✡ ❋ ✳

4. ✳ ✜ ✜ ✳ ★

5. ✜ ✷ ✜ ☆ ✡ ✳ ★ ✜ ✳

6. ✜ ✷ ✜ ◉ ❋ ☆ ✪ ✳

ALL CHANGE

Scientific experiments are all about changes. In these puzzles you are changing the top word into the bottom word by replacing one letter at a time. We give you some clues to help you along.

1. In outer space there are extremes of heat and cold.

    Change HEAT into COLD.

H E A T

— — — —   Top of the body

— — — —   Grasped something tightly

— — — —   This word follows strong to mean a fort

C O L D

2. Prepare to LAND from outer space to HERE!

L A N D

— — — —   It's at the end of the arm

— — — —   Opposite of soft

— — — —   Group of cows

H E R E

SPACE FACTS

The first rockets were created as early as the 10th century in China, where they were initially used as weapons in battle.

Geostationary orbits are when satellites are placed in an orbit 22,236 miles (35,785 kilometres) above the equator and remain in a fixed position above a certain point on Earth's surface.

SpaceX has developed the world's first fully reusable rocket. The two-stage vessel, which is made up of the Super Heavy booster and Starship spacecraft, is the largest and most powerful launch vehicle ever created, and is planned to play a key role in returning astronauts to the Moon – and possibly even to Mars!

SEEING DOUBLE

Astronauts sometimes suffered with problems with their eyesight after returning to Earth. Scientists worked in space to see if they could find out more about this.

You are not seeing double in this puzzle, but you do have two crossword grids, Grid A and Grid B, which are the same. There are also two sets of clues. The answer to 3 across in Grid A is CHECK. You now have to work out which grid the rest of the answers f it into.

ACROSS

3. Make sure everything is OK / Our planet (5)

6. Take exercise outside the space capsule / Keep in your hand (4)

7. A day-to-day record of what you did / Doze, especially at night (5)

8. Tiny black insects / Small green vegetables (4)

10. The Atlantic or Pacific / Moved quickly to win a competition (5)

14. A satellite _ _ _ _ is a type of aerial / Connected things that show what you have to do (4)

15. The universe beyond our planet, _ _ _ _ space / Watery air in the sky (5)

16. Repair / Item of footwear (4)

17. Constellation of Gemini / Open and close your eyes quickly (5)

DOWN

1. Perspire, lose water through the skin / This follows space to mean rockets or vehicles (5)
2. A dwarf planet or a Disney dog / A sky without 15 across (5)
4. Creature, such as a dog or a monkey / Gave assistance or support (6)
5. Team on board a spacecraft / Move in another direction (4)
9. Planet with rings / It shows words and pictures on a laptop (6)
11. Enters a pool head first / Hours of darkness (5)
12. Strong metal / Out of the Sun (5)
13. Travelled in a plane or spacecraft / Oil, gas, petrol etc. that powers a vehicle (4)

GRID A

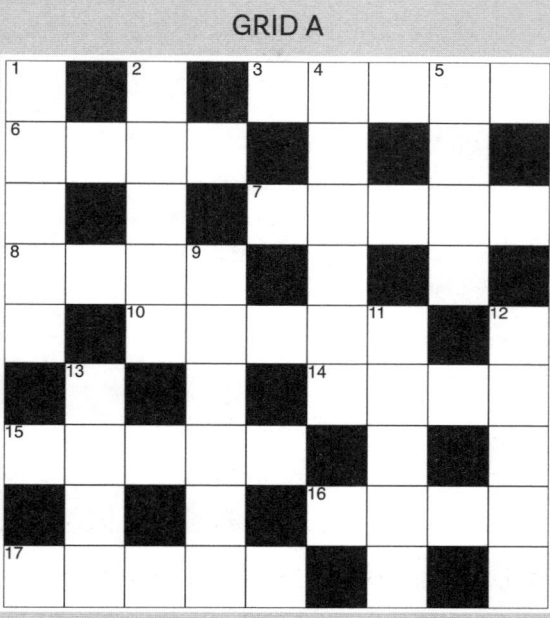

GRID B

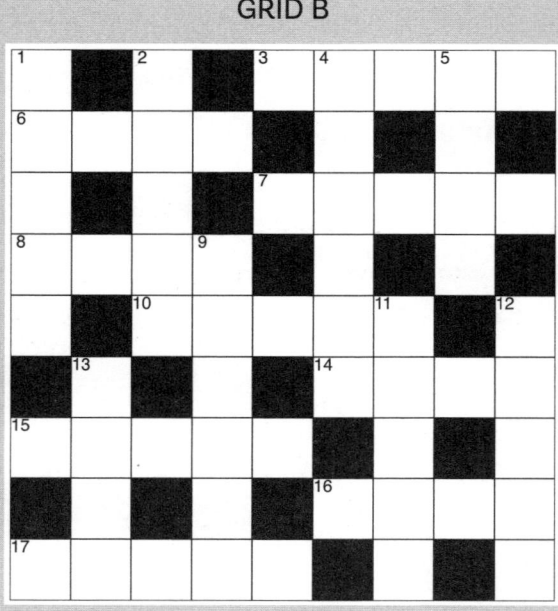

PEGGY WHITSON

One of the most influential figures in modern space travel is American astronaut Peggy Whitson. Whitson's fascination with space began at a young age when, aged nine, she watched the events of the Apollo 11 Moon landing unfold on television at her family's farm in Iowa. This led her to dedicate herself to studying science, and she would later graduate from university with a Bachelor of Science degree in biology and chemistry, followed later by a doctorate degree in biochemistry.

Whitson began working at NASA in the late 1980s as a National Research Council Resident Research Associate, focusing on biomedical and biochemical research. In this role, she played an important part in developing and working on some of the experiments that NASA would send to space aboard the Space Shuttle, and Russian Mir space station when the US formed closer ties with their former Space Race rivals.

In 1996 Whitson would achieve her goal of being selected as an astronaut candidate. She would complete two years of rigorous training and subsequently play a key role in ground-based astronaut operations. Finally, in June 2002, she would fulfil her dream of travelling to space when she was selected to be Flight Engineer 1 as part of Expedition 5, a programme that saw the International Space Station (ISS) being permanently occupied and crews remaining aboard for extended periods of time. Whitson would spend a total of 184 days in space as part of this mission, six aboard the Space Shuttle *Endeavour* and an incredible 178 aboard the ISS.

Whitson would return to the ISS in 2007 as part of Expedition 16, which saw her spend a further 192 days in space, and then again in 2016 for Expedition 50, remaining aboard for Expedition 51 (in which she took the role of mission commander) and 52 for a total of 289 days aboard the station. In the process, she would break the record as the oldest woman to fly in space (at the age of 56) and became the American astronaut to have spent the most time in space, having amassed a total of 665 days for her various NASA missions upon her return to Earth in September 2017. Across the five Expedition missions to which she was assigned, Whitson took part in an incredible ten spacewalks, making her one of the most experienced extra-vehicular activity specialists.

Whitson retired from NASA in 2018, but this didn't mark the end of her time in space: she subsequently began working for Axiom Space, a privately owned commercial spaceflight company, and in 2023 she took the role of commander for Axiom Mission 2, which visited the ISS for eight days. Whitson's determination to fulfil her childhood dream of travelling to space has made her one of the most experienced astronauts in history, whose place in the story of human spaceflight is every bit as inspiring as the Apollo 11 astronauts she had admired in her childhood.

SHAPE UP

For an experiment, you need to make a solid cube from a flat piece of card. A cube is a solid shape with six square faces or sides.

Which of these shapes could be used to form a cube?

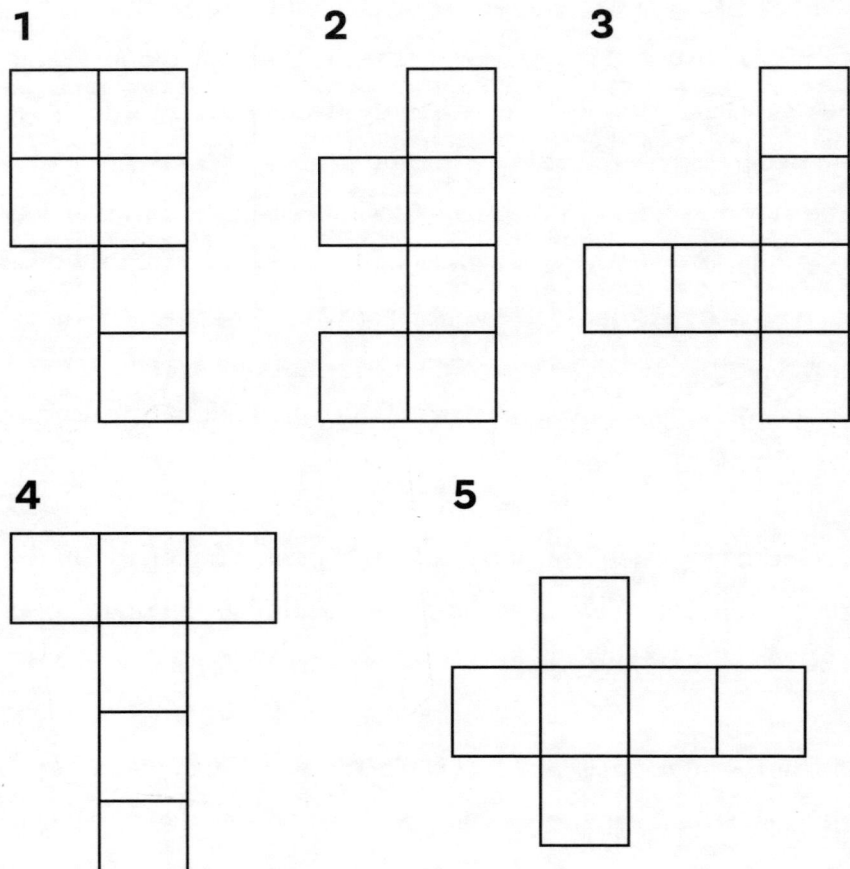

1

2

3

4

5

BOXING CLEVER

We have managed to make our solid cube. Here's an empty box. In a scientific experiment it is important to look at every option when running a trial and recording data. How many ways are there of placing the cube into the box so that it is always in a different position?

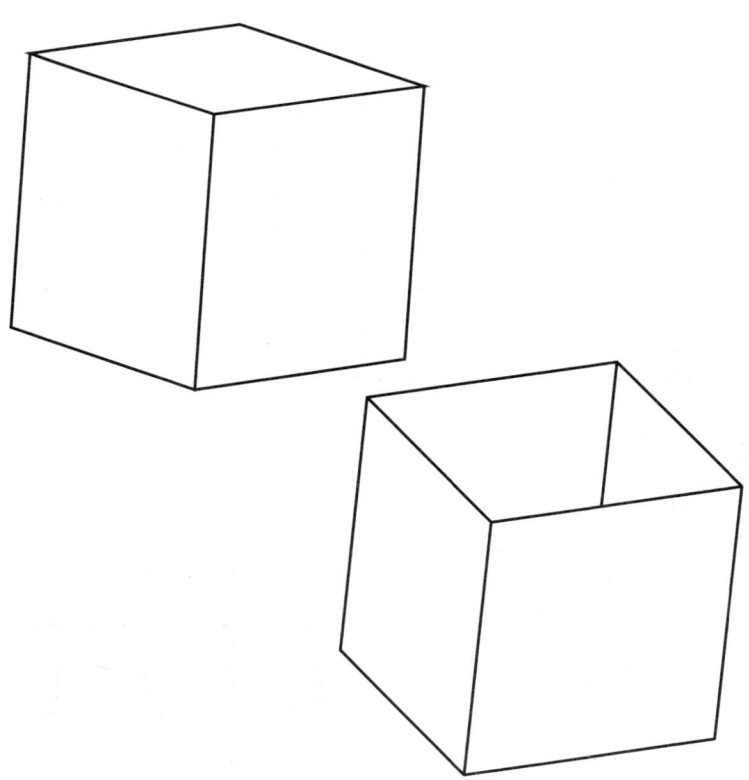

MIXED MENU

The commands on the menu bar on the computer have had their letters muddled up. Sort them out and set out the instructions for the astronauts to follow.

1. VASE _____

2. LIFE _____

3. HEARS _____

4. TIDE _____

5. INTERS _____

6. UPSET _____ _____ (two words)

7. ELECTS _____

8. CLARE _____

9. TAPES _____

10. WARD _____

PASSCODE

You must know the passcode in order to be able to access the computer and all the information you need to carry out your work in space. Work out which numbers go in each of the blank spaces so that every row, every column and every diagonal adds up to 30. The passcode is the numbers that go across in the middle row, which is currently completely blank. It is made up of FIVE digits in total.

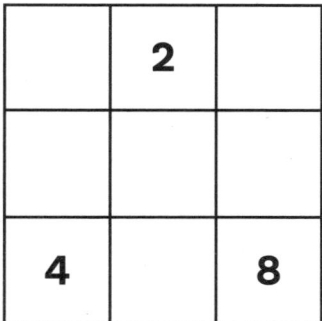

7. EXTRA-TERRESTRIAL LIFE

For centuries, humans have looked up at the skies and wondered if there are other life forms out there looking back. Extra-terrestrial life forms – also known as aliens – might seem like pure science fiction, but scientists today are seriously looking for signs of life on other planets, moons and asteroids. Rather than little green men in flying saucers, this search covers everything from microscopic bacteria, simple animals or plants, right up to intelligent beings.

Philosophers and scholars have long speculated about what other worlds might be capable of supporting life, human or otherwise. As techniques developed, astronomers noticed that the laws of physics appeared to be the same everywhere, and that Earth wasn't necessarily a special case. In the 18th century, Sir Isaac Newton's theory of gravity strengthened this view, explaining mathematically why planets orbit around stars, and raising questions about what other planets might be out there. In the late 19th century, some astronomers were sure they could see canals on the surface of Mars, and speculation grew that these were evidence of a Martian civilisation. It later turned out that these 'canals' were actually an optical illusion, caused by poor-quality telescopes.

Today, many space missions feature experiments to look for signs of life. There's no reason that life on other planets would be similar to life on Earth – it could live in very different conditions, be based on completely different elements and go through entirely different processes. This makes it very difficult to search for alien life, because we essentially don't know what to look for or where to look for it. However, we do know that life is possible where there is plenty of liquid water, an oxygen-rich atmosphere and an abundance of carbon, because these conditions form the basis for life on Earth. This gives scientists a way to narrow down the search and explains why most searches for alien life begin by looking for water. Traces have been found elsewhere, but so far, Earth is the only place known to have stable bodies of water.

Soon, that may change. In 2023, the European Space Agency launched a robotic spacecraft to search for liquid water and signs of life on three of Jupiter's moons. The Jupiter Icy Moons Explorer, also known as *Juice*, will reach Jupiter in 2031, where it will orbit the moons Ganymede, Callisto and Europa. The surfaces of these moons are almost completely frozen, giving scientists hope that there might be liquid oceans beneath the ice that are capable of supporting life.

While many space missions are looking for signs of life, there is also an active community here on Earth involved in the search. The main research organisation involved in this is the SETI (Search for Extraterrestrial Intelligence), Institute which was founded in 1984. Space is full of signals, emitted by bodies such as stars as they radiate energy, and telescopes and receivers on Earth can pick these up. The SETI Institute focuses on analysing the signals for any that stand out – for example, those that may contain patterns that look intentional.

While believing in aliens and UFOs may be controversial, most scientists believe there is a good chance that life exists in some form beyond Earth, enough to undertake serious research to find it. Are we alone in the universe? And if not, will it be life as we know it, or something beyond our imaginations?

SHADOW PLAY

Answer the clues and write your answers going across in the large grid. When this grid is complete, take the letters in the shaded squares and write them in the numbered spaces going down in the smaller grid. The first shady letters you will write are C with O underneath it. When this lower grid is full, you should be able to split the letters up into words that complete a famous quotation from a film. The quotation begins:
'In space, no one...'

CLUES

1. It tells you the time
2. This is when you stop what you are doing, then start again
3. Planet that is closest in size to its neighbour Earth
4. An opening or door in a spacecraft
5. A mistake or fault
6. Band of fire seen below a rocket when it is launched
7. Astronauts drink through one to combat microgravity
8. Words that sound the same at the end like MARS and STARS are said to do this

	1	2	3	4	5	6	7	8
	C							
	O							

In space, no one _ _ _   _ _ _ _   _ _ _   _ _ _ _ _ _

WHO AM I?

Who is this visitor from outer space? Look at the clues and work out which letters you need to spell out its name.

My first is in Moon,

But isn't in one.

My second's in age,

But isn't in gone.

My third is in rings,

But isn't in sing.

My fourth is in tiring,

But isn't in ring.

My fifth is in ice,

But isn't in space.

My sixth is in air,

And also in place.

My last is in wind,

But isn't in wide.

Please visit my planet,

Come along for the ride.

Who am I?

STRANGE SIGNS

What are these strange signs? Is it a form of communication from another world? Do the images convey a message? Do they mean anything?

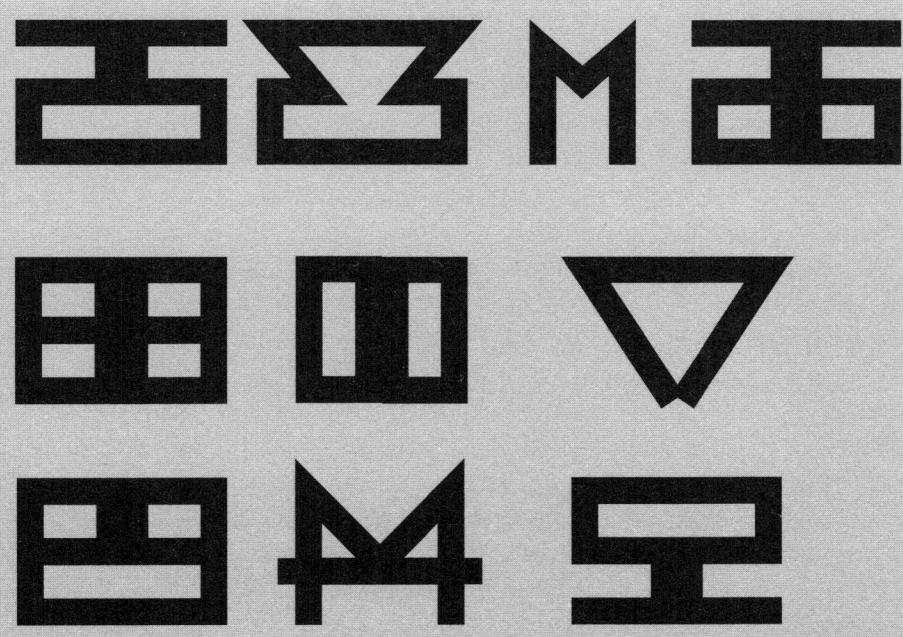

ALAN SHEPARD

The world was stunned in April 1961 when the Soviet Union announced that it had sent Yuri Gagarin to space and safely returned him to Earth. The United States, a pioneer in so many new and emerging technologies of the era, suddenly found itself behind in the Space Race – but it would not be long before they followed in the footsteps of the Russians and also put a human being in space, in the process making Alan Shepard a hero.

Alan Bartlett Shepard Jr. was born in November 1923. He excelled at school, but young Shepard's heart was set on the skies. He was fascinated by aircraft, and as a teenager would help out at a nearby airfield in exchange for flights in aeroplanes where he was occasionally allowed to take the controls himself.

The United States' entry into World War II changed everything, however, and eager to play his part, Shepard enlisted in the US Navy, eventually being stationed at a Naval Air Station where he trained as a pilot – and it is this that led to him being put forward in 1959 as a candidate for the Mercury space program, which was charged with putting the first American in space. His launch aboard the *Freedom 7* spacecraft took place on May 5, 1961 – less than a month after Gagarin's historic flight. Unlike his Russian counterpart, Shepard didn't orbit Earth, and his flight lasted just 15 minutes, in comparison to Gagarin's almost two-hour mission.

Shepard was subsequently selected to take part in the Gemini programme that followed Mercury, but in 1963 he began to suffer from an inner ear disorder that would prevent him from flying again until 1969. When his flight worthiness was finally restored, Shepard was assigned a place on the Apollo programme, and in early 1971 commanded Apollo 14 on a mission to the Moon. In doing so, he became, at the age of 47, the oldest man ever to walk on the Moon, and the only member of the Mercury program to travel there. He also took part in another historic moment during this mission when he became the first person to ever hit a golf ball on the Moon!

Alan Shepard retired from the US space agency NASA in 1974, three years after his moonwalk, but space would always play a role in his life: in the 1980s, he would co-found the Mercury Seven Foundation, a non-profit organisation that provided college scholarships in science and engineering subjects. To this day an annual award, the Alan Shepard Technology in Education Award, is named for him and given to teachers in the United States who excel in applying technology to aid their students.

THE MAN IN THE MOON

Looking at a full Moon from Earth, it can appear that it has the features of a human face. Many cultures have tales about the 'Man in the Moon'. In the moons shown here, numbers form the features of the face. If all the numbers were added together, which moon would have the highest total?

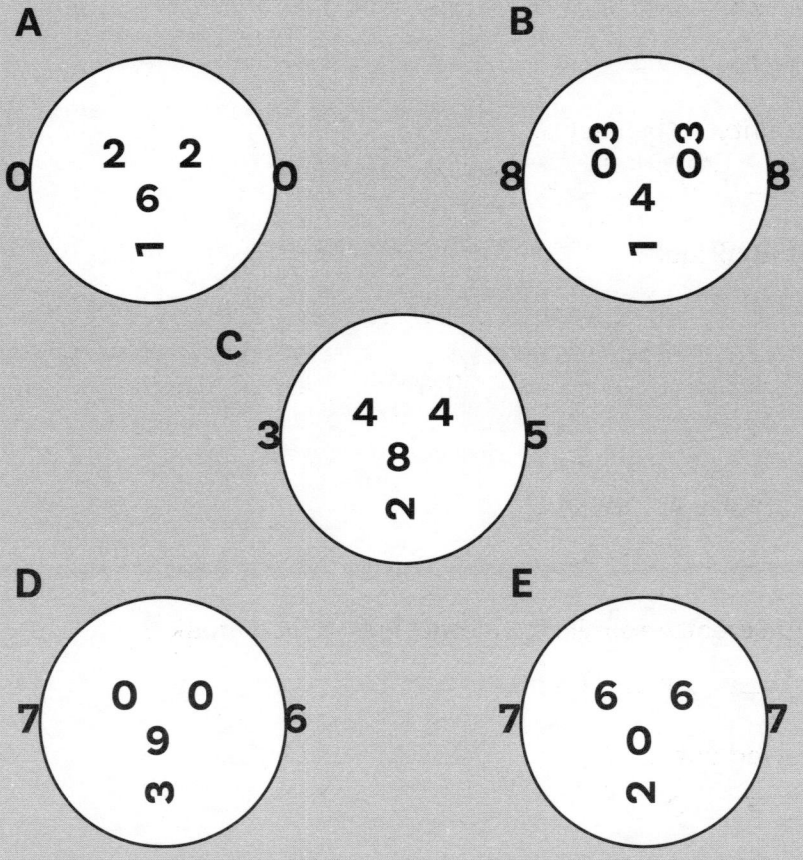

UFO

A UFO is an Unidentified Flying Object. Is it from another planet? Where has it come from? Where is it going to? In this puzzle we give you clues to words that contain the letters U, F and O in that order. We also give you the letters U, F and O to help you work out the answers.

1 Special clothes you wear to school

U _ _ F O _ _

2 A very heavy type of cattle, also called a bison

_ U F _ _ _ O

3 A county in the east of England

_ U _ F O _ _

4 Not at all lucky

U _ F O _ _ _ _ _ _ _

5 Opened out, as you might do with a large piece of paper

U _ F O _ _ _ _

6 Where you are walking

U _ _ _ _ F O _ _

7 Large creature similar to a toad, with a loud croak

_ U _ _ F _ O _

8 Thawed out

U _ F _ O _ _

MYSTERY MESSAGE

Look at the computer keyboard. The top row is made up of digits 1 to 0. There are three lines of letters underneath these digits. Beneath number are the letters Q, A and Z. Beneath 2 are the letters W, S and X, and so on. 8 has just I and K, while 9 has just O and L. Beneath 0 there is just P.

Using the picture of the keyboard, can you work out the message? Your skill is needed to choose which of the letters below a number is the letter that is needed.

ALIEN TERRITORY

Three aliens, Xenon, Yttrium and Zirconium, have to move from their danger area D to their safe area S. Their only way to do this is via a unique ray. At least one individual must be travelling every time the ray is used, but only two individuals can travel at once.

Xenon feels it is too dangerous to travel with, or be left alone with, Yttrium. Yttrium feels it is too dangerous to travel with, or be left alone with, Zirconium. Zirconium has agreed to travel with either of the other aliens.

It is up to you to take these three aliens to a place of safety. How would you plan the journeys to make sure Xenon, Yttrium and Zirconium all travel with you safely and all reach the safety of S?

Remember, Xenon and Yttrium cannot be left together on their own and nor can Yttrium and Zirconium.

HELEN SHARMAN

The chance to give up your job and train to be an astronaut is a dream that many people would wish for – and for Helen Sharman (born in 1963) it actually came true! 1963 also happens to be the same year that Valentina Tereshkova became the first woman in space.

Project Juno, a joint venture between Soviet Russia and the UK, was planned in the 1980s to promote closer ties between the two countries and to put the first British person in space. Sharman, a 27-year-old chemist who was, at the time, working for confectionary company Mars, leapt at the opportunity after hearing an advert on the radio saying, 'Astronaut wanted: no experience necessary', and was subsequently picked from amongst 13,000 applicants.

Sharman moved to the Star City space training centre just outside Moscow in Russia, where she would learn all the skills she would need for her trip to space, including everything from preparing for the rocket launch, how to function in the micro-gravity environment of the Soviet Mir space station and how to conduct a series of experiments aboard the station – all while learning to speak Russian at the same time!

The Soyuz rocket carrying Sharman blasted off on 18 May 1991 – in the process making her the first British astronaut, and the first woman from Western Europe, to travel to space. She lived aboard Mir for eight days, carrying out a number of scientific experiments, taking photographs of the UK from orbit and even talking to British schoolchildren via radio about her experience of being in space.

Since returning to Earth, Sharman has continued to play a key role in promoting British interests in space flight through radio and television appearances and public speaking events, and you can see the space suit she wore on her historic mission on display at the Science Museum!

EXTRA LINK

The pairs of words in this puzzle have a link with the cosmos beyond our own atmosphere. They are not linked by meaning but are still linked. The last letters of the first word are the first of the next. When you have found all the links that complete the words, search them out in the word search grid. They can go in any direction, across, backwards, up, down or diagonally.

1 O Z O _ _   _ _ P T U N E

2 M E T E _ _   _ _ B I T

3 S _ _   _ _ I V E R S E

4 J U P I _ _ _   _ _ _ R E S T R I A L

5 N A _ _   _ _ T U R N

6 A S T R O N O _ _ _   _ _ _ C U R Y

7 E A R _ _   _ _ E O R Y

8 O B S E R _ _   _ _ N U S

```
J U P I T E R P S P Y A
S O J L N P S U N R L S
A E U O M O N E R A Y T
T S Z N M E E U I U S R
U O J M V E P R G N P O
R R B R X E T U O I R N
N B G S R S U E N V I O
U I R D E S N N O E N M
R T A R H R E B A R G E
D S R D R E V Q U S I R
M E R C U R Y E H E A P
T H E O R Y J H T R A E
```

SPACE FACTS

The first private space flight was on 21 June 2004, when pilot Mike Melvill flew *SpaceShipOne* to space, in the process of becoming the first commercial pilot-astronaut.

Launching a rocket into space is incredibly expensive – every launch costs millions of pounds.

The first spacewalk took place on 18 March 1965, when Soviet cosmonaut Alexei Leonov spent a little over 12 minutes outside his Voskhod spacecraft. The United States conducted their first spacewalk three months later in June 1965.

THE VISITORS

Imagine what it would be like to have an E.T. visitor from space calling at your house! During the years when the Space Race captured the imagination of the general public, British comics featured stories about friendly alien visitors. There was Jimmi from Jupiter, Vanessa from Venus and Jack Flash from Mercury. In the early 1980s, Steven Spielberg created the ultimate extra-terrestrial adventure in his movie *E.T. The Extra-Terrestrial*.

As part of a school project on space, a class has been asked to create a fantasy adventure about a visiting alien. Harry, Jade and Lewis have come up with some out-of-this-world ideas. They have each given their visitor a name, and given them a special super-power.

Can you complete the grid and work out what is going on in the storylines?

Read all the clues carefully, then write a tick (✓) in any square in the grid when you know two pieces of information can be linked together. Write a cross (✗) in any square when you are sure that two pieces of information cannot be linked. Whenever you write a tick then two crosses can go in the remaining squares in the row of three squares in a box. Also, two crosses can go in the remaining squares in the column of three squares in a box.

CLUES

Harry's alien didn't have a name containing a number.

Lewis's alien was not the one who could read minds.

Phobos could make himself invisible.

Jade's alien was called Ganymede.

| | | Alien Names | | | Superpower | | |
		Ganymede	Phobos	Smosh7	Can Fly	Reads Minds	Turns Invisible
Story Writer	Harry						
	Jade						
	Lewis						
Superpower	Can Fly						
	Reads Minds						
	Turns Invisible						

SPACE FACTS

If you fell into a black hole, the intense gravitational forces would stretch you out. Scientists have given this phenomenon the name 'spaghettification'.

The biggest threat to spacecraft, space stations and satellites are the thousands of pieces of space junk floating around in orbit. From tiny pieces of metal to larger, non-functional satellites, these objects can travel at up to 22,000 miles per hour (35,000 km/h), meaning that even the smallest thing can pose a massive risk to astronauts and spaceships!

Abandon Earth! In about 7.5 billion years our Sun will expand so much that it will swallow Earth.

CIPHER FROM SPACE

This message has been received from outer space. The senders have created a code with numbers that are familiar to us. There are 26 letters in our alphabet. There are 26 numbers in the code, which follows a definite pattern. The number 26 replaces the letter A. The number 22 replaces the letter E. Can you crack the code and work out what the message is?

21. 9. 18. 22. 13. 23. 8.

24. 26. 13.   2. 12. 6.   9. 22. 26. 23.   12. 6. 9.

14. 22. 8. 8. 26. 20. 22.?

19. 26. 5. 22.   4. 22.   20. 12. 7.   18. 7.   9. 18. 20. 19. 7.?

Here's our alphabet.
Use this as a checklist as you crack the code.

A	B	C	D	E	F	G	H	I	J	K	L	M
26	_	_	_	22	_	_	_	_	_	_	_	_

N	O	P	Q	R	S	T	U	V	W	X	Y	Z
—	—	—	—	—	—	—	—	—	—	—	—	—

SPACE FACTS

Distances in space are measured in Astronomical Units (AUs – the distance between Earth and the Sun) and light years (how far light travels in one Earth year). One AU is about 93 million miles, while one light year is a whopping 5,900,000,000,000 miles!

The galaxy we live in, the Milky Way, measures about 105,700 light years across!

Moon dust is a type of loose rock and dust called regolith that can also be found here on Earth and on Mars!

Jupiter's moon Ganymede is the largest satellite in the Solar System – it's even bigger than the planet Mercury!

ODD ORDER

Here are some book titles about space and the possibility of extra-terrestrial life.

1. IS ANYONE OUT THERE?

2. THE FIRST WOMAN FROM GANYMEDE

3. HAZARDS WITH RE-ENTRY INTO EARTH'S ATMOSPHERE

4. UFO URGENTLY NEEDED!

5. IF I VENTURE BEYOND MARS

There is a reason that these titles are in this order. Can you work out what it is?

Tip 1: The answer is nothing to do with facts about space.

Tip 2: Numbers are involved, but no calculations are needed!

THE APOLLO 11 ASTRONAUTS

Three names are perhaps more well known than any others when looking at the history of human space flight: Neil Armstrong, Buzz Aldrin and Michael Collins – the first men on the Moon.

The three men that would make up the Apollo 11 crew were all experienced astronauts by the time they were chosen to take part in the first mission to the Moon's surface, having already flown in the Gemini programme of the mid-1960s – Armstrong on Gemini 8, Collins on Gemini 10 and Aldrin on Gemini 12 – and it was their expertise there that would make them the perfect candidates to fulfil President John F. Kennedy's goal of 'landing a man on the Moon and returning him safely to Earth.'

Launching on 16 July 1969, Apollo 11 took around three days to travel from Earth to the Moon. Once in orbit, Armstrong and Aldrin moved to the lunar module, named *Eagle*, that would carry them to the Moon's surface. Collins, meanwhile, was left aboard the command module in orbit of the Moon for the duration of the time his crewmates were on the lunar surface – and out of radio contact with Earth for almost 50 minutes every time the spaceship rounded the far side of the Moon. He nevertheless said that he didn't feel isolated or alone, and simply carried on with his work maintaining the vessel that would ultimately take the three astronauts home.

Armstrong and Aldrin, meanwhile, would land on the Moon's surface, Armstrong informing mission control that they had set down safely by stating, 'the *Eagle* has landed'. Almost three hours after landing, Armstrong would be the first of the two astronauts to leave the lunar module, descending *Eagle*'s ladder and planting humanity's first footsteps on the Moon's dusty surface. He would mark the occasion by saying words that would go down in history: 'That's one small step for [a] man, one giant leap for mankind.' A short time later, Buzz Aldrin would join him on the surface, the two men recording footage of the 'magnificent desolation', as Aldrin would describe it, collecting samples to return to Earth for scientific analysis, and planting a stars and stripes flag to mark their historic mission.

Apollo 11 would be on the Moon's surface for just 21 hours – far shorter than the missions that followed – and, after a successful lunar launch, would rendezvous with the orbiting command module and fellow astronaut Michael Collins, ready to begin the voyage home. The three men would return to Earth on 24 July, where they would be celebrated worldwide for their historic mission. The command module that safely carried them to the moon and back was subsequently put on display at the National Air and Space Museum in Washington DC, where it remains to this day as a symbol of human ingenuity.

PLANET PROBES

Space probes are unmanned devices sent to explore space and gather scientific information.

These probes are destined to pass planets in our Solar System. Symbols replace letters as a security code measure. The symbols remain constant throughout. The first set of symbols stands for MARS. Which planets are the other probes going to investigate?

1.   ^   *   %   &
      M   A   R   S

2.   &   * $ £   %   !

    _ _ _ _ _ _

3.   £   %   *   !   £   &

    _ _ _ _ _ _

4.   !   ?   @ $ £   !   ?

    _ _ _ _ _ _ _

SPACE FACTS

There are two types of spacewalk – tethered, where the astronaut is physically connected to their spacecraft, and untethered, where no connection is used. Untethered walks carry more risk as there's a chance that the astronaut could float off into space! As a result, they have only been performed a handful of times.

The first untethered spacewalk was performed by Bruce McCandless in 1984. McCandless was the first astronaut to use NASA's Manned Manoeuvring Unit (MMU) which allowed him to travel away from the Space Shuttle *Challenger* and be photographed hanging alone in orbit above Earth. It was eventually decided that the MMU offered no real advantage over tethered spacewalks, and in fact posed greater risk to astronauts, so it was retired.

8. WHAT'S NEXT?

When we look at the space missions of today, it's hard to believe the dawn of the Space Age is still in living memory. In less than a century, we've gone from the first human-made object in space to space stations, space-tourism and robots on Mars. In that time, over 5,000 rockets have been launched, more than 600 people have been to space, and 12 have even walked on the Moon. Space activity is showing no sign of slowing down. In fact, the global space sector is growing like never before, with countless companies and space agencies launching their own missions. Scientists and engineers keep pushing the boundaries of what's possible by developing new technologies, resulting in more advanced and sophisticated missions that can reach even deeper into space.

One of these distant targets is our neighbour, Mars. While it's our nearest planet, it isn't exactly close – it takes around three days for astronauts to travel to the Moon, but according to NASA, it would take around nine months to reach Mars. We don't have the technology to do this yet, so scientists are developing new ways of using robotic technology to investigate the Red Planet. In 2021, NASA's *Perseverance* rover touched down on Mars. About the size of a small car, *Perseverance* is driving around the Martian surface, sending images back to Earth and collecting rock samples. These samples are deposited at designated pickup points, to be collected and returned to Earth by a future mission. Using a probe or rover to collect data on a target is useful, but being able to retrieve actual samples and analyse them on Earth is even more valuable. Once the scientists have the sample, they can subject it to as many tests as they want. Analysing samples from Mars will revolutionise what we know about its history, whether it's ever been home to life, and help pave the way for future missions.

These robotic missions aren't a complete substitute for human astronauts, however. Astronauts have a variety of responsibilities: their mission might have one main goal, but they can take readings and make observations, perform experiments, carry out repairs and maintenance, and communicate and work as a team. Crewed missions are still vital for space exploration, and off-world bases will be key for missions reaching further out into the Solar System, to Mars and beyond. Within the next few years, NASA will send astronauts back to the Moon for the first time since 1972 as part of a plan to create a permanent human presence there. Astronauts in the Artemis programme will explore how to live and work sustainably on the Moon, generating energy and making use of its resources, while also investigating what the Moon can tell us about the history of Earth.

Space exploration has always been ambitious, achieving what was thought to be impossible and overcoming obstacles with ever-advancing technology. Over a million people work in the space industry worldwide, from administrators and project managers to engineers and astronauts. All these people are playing their part in missions that will see the first woman of colour on the Moon and put the first disabled astronaut in space. Maybe in the future, you'll have your part to play, too.

SPACE FACTS

Earth isn't the only place where water exists; both our Moon and Mars hold reserves of water, while three of Jupiter's moons – Europa, Ganymede and Callisto – and two of Saturn's – Enceladus and Titan – are thought to possess underwater oceans. Incredibly, scientists believe that these oceans might even be home to some form of underwater life!

Venus and Uranus spin in the opposite direction to all the other planets in the Solar System – and scientists have no idea why!

NASA sent a helicopter to the planet Mars! Called *Ingenuity*, this plucky little chopper made its first flight in April 2021 and spent almost three years exploring the Martian skies before its mission ended in January 2024.

YANG LIWEI

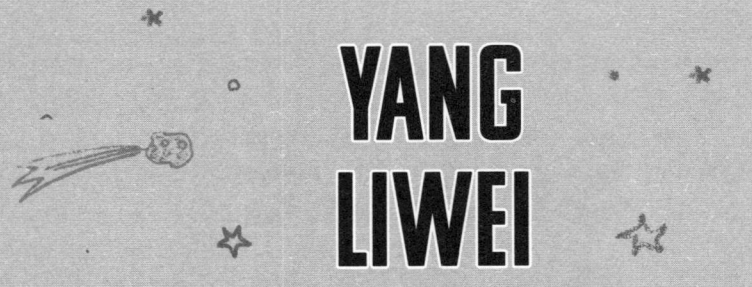

For decades, two nations have dominated humanity's efforts in space: the United States and the former Soviet Union. But in the 21st century, more countries have taken their first steps into space, with China the third to do so.

China's first crewed mission to space took place on 15 October 2003, when then-Lt. Colonel Yang Liwei (b. 1965) was launched into space aboard *Shenzhou 5* from a launch pad in the Gobi Desert, and in the process became the country's first taikonaut (the Chinese equivalent of an American or European astronaut or Russian cosmonaut). Liwei was an experienced air force pilot at the time he was chosen for China's space programme in 1998, and was one of 11 recruits selected from among 1500 candidates. He subsequently underwent a comprehensive program of training that incorporated physical and psychological conditioning as well as learning scientific principles that would influence his mission, and how to operate the craft that would carry him into space.

Liwei's mission would be relatively short – he would spend just 21 hours in space across 14 orbits of Earth – but the ramifications of his mission were huge: in the years that have followed, China has established itself as a major player in the field of space exploration, conducting its first spacewalks, sending probes to the Moon and Mars and launching its own space station in permanent Earth orbit.

In the wake of his mission, Liwei was the recipient of numerous awards, including the title of 'Space Hero' from the Chinese military and the Medal of Space Science from the United Nations Educational, Scientific and Cultural Organisation, while Russia awarded him the Gagarin Medal named in honour of the first human in space. Like Yuri Gagarin, Liwei has not flown again in space since his historic mission; instead, he was given the role of vice-commander-in-chief of the astronauts system of China's crewed spaceflight project, ensuring that he continues to play a role in his country's future space endeavours.

THE COSMOS

In this puzzle you are looking at the whole cosmos, where everything is linked together. Can you fit all the listed names into the grid? Words read either across or down. Four letters are in place to start you off. There is only one possible solution.

3 LETTERS
SUN

4 LETTERS
ERIS
MARS
MOON
STAR

5 LETTERS
CERES
COMET
EARTH
ORION
PLUTO
TITAN
VENUS

6 LETTERS
GEMINI
HAUMEA
NEBULA
PULSAR
SATURN
URANUS

7 LETTERS
JUPITER
MERCURY
NEPTUNE

8 LETTERS
ASTEROID
GALAXIES
MAKEMAKE
MILKY WAY

9 LETTERS
ANDROMEDA
METEORITE
METEOROID
THE PLOUGH
URSA MAJOR

10 LETTERS
TRIANGULUM

13 LETTERS
CONSTELLATION

U

G

E

N

SPACE FACTS

Is there life on Mars? Scientists have long believed that the Red Planet is the most likely place in the Solar System outside of Earth to harbour life, especially since water – vital for the formation of life – has been discovered on the planet's surface.

Astronaut James Young has flown on more types of spacecraft than anyone else: Gemini, Apollo command module, Apollo lunar lander and the Space Shuttle.

Apollo 13 holds the record of the crewed spaceship that travelled the furthest distance from Earth. On 15 April 1970 it passed the dark side of the Moon at a distance of 248,655 miles.

LUNAR LOTTERY

Holidays in space used to be found only in stories of science fiction. However, they might be closer than you think.

Five friends have all bought a lottery ticket and the top prize is a trip to outer space. Can you work out the name of each person, and the number of their lottery ticket?

Girl A says, 'My ticket has three numbers that are all the same. Venus's ticket has the lowest number.'

Boy B says, 'My ticket has a 6 on it. My name's not Ray.'

Girl C says, 'Star is the only one of us who doesn't have a number 3 on her ticket.'

Girl D says, 'My ticket is 730, which is higher than Leo's.'

Boy E says, 'The numbers on my ticket are the same as Miranda's, but they are in a different order.'

When you have worked out who has which ticket, work out the winner. It's the person with the ticket where the three digits add up to the lowest number.

SPACE FACTS

The first mammal in space was a rhesus monkey called Albert II, who was launched aboard a US V2 rocket on 14 June 1947.

A wide variety of animals have travelled to space, from dogs and primates to mice, fruit flies, meal worms and even two Russian tortoises!

The oldest human-made object in space is the US satellite *Vanguard 1*. Launched in 1958, the satellite stopped functioning in 1964 but continues to circle Earth to this day.

Nebulas are vast clouds of dust and gas in space that can measure hundreds of light years across.

TEXT TRICKSTERS

Can you work out what each text trickster means?

1.

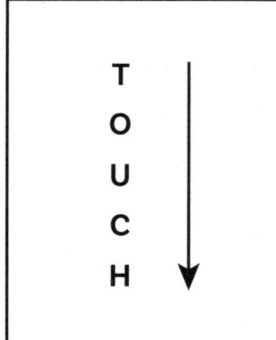

2.

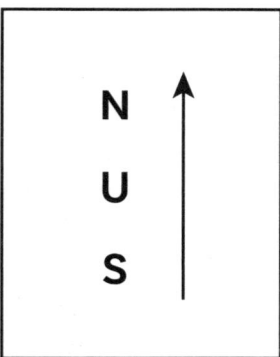

3.

HTЯAƎ OT

4.

SPA**LOST**CE

5.

WILLIAM SHATNER

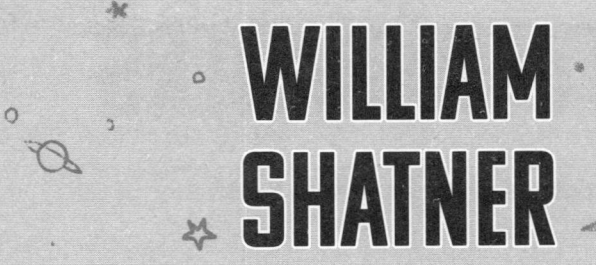

Actor, author, entertainer and pop-culture icon William Shatner has been a familiar figure across the entertainment industry for decades, but in 2021 he added another string to his bow: astronaut.

Born in 1931, Shatner is best known for his role as Captain James T. Kirk in the original *Star Trek* television series that ran from 1966 to 1969, and the first seven *Star Trek* films, beginning with *Star Trek: The Motion Picture* in 1979. But after a lifetime spent as one of science-fiction's most well-known space adventurers, Shatner was offered the chance to travel to space for real when he was approached by Jeff Bezos' private space flight company Blue Origin.

The opportunity to boldly go where only his fictional alter-ego had gone before was one that Shatner leapt at – and at the age of 90, it would make him at the time the oldest person ever to travel to space. Shatner boarded the *New Shepard* rocket, named for pioneering NASA astronaut Alan Shepard, at Blue Origins' West Texas launch site on 13 October 2021, alongside fellow space tourists Glen de Vries, Chris Boshuizen and Audrey Powers. Their flight aboard the fully automated rocket would last a little over ten minutes and see them travel to the Kármán Line, which is regarded as being the very edge of space. There, for just a few minutes, they experienced the sensation of weightlessness and the sight of our home planet hanging in the vastness of space, before descending back to Earth.

For Shatner, the experience of seeing Earth from space was a life-changing one: the excitement he had as the launch got under way would soon give way to unexpected sadness and what he would describe as 'the strongest feelings of grief' as he contemplated the fragility of our planet. This phenomenon – an intense, awe-inspiring sensation that comes from seeing Earth from space – is not unusual among astronauts, and was named the 'Overview Effect' by space philosopher Frank White.

While some would dismiss Shatner's flight as a mere publicity stunt, the actor himself insisted that 'everyone' should have the opportunity to experience what he did for the greater good of humanity. And with the era of space tourism only just beginning, the reality is that more people will have that remarkable opportunity in the future.

NEXT, PLEASE!

The puzzles in this section look to the future. Here is a list of words with some of their letters missing. Those letters are all found in the word NEXT. Letters can be used more than once in a word and you might not need every letter in every word. The letters N, E, X and T can be used in any order. We give you a clue each time.

1. P L A _ _ _ (Mercury, Saturn or Venus, for example)

2. _ _ P _ U _ _ (another example of answer 1)

3. U _ I V _ R S _ (the cosmos)

4. O _ Y G _ _ (gas which makes up about 20 per cent of Earth's atmosphere)

5. _ _ G I _ _ _ R (skilled mechanic or technician who works in or on spacecraft)

6. _ _ L _ S C O P _ (invented by Galileo and makes distant objects seem nearer)

7. _ _ W _ O _ (scientist Isaac famous for his work on gravity)

8. _ I _ S _ _ I _ (another scientist Albert, one of the greatest of the 20th century)

9. _ _ P _ D I _ I O _ (a journey of exploration)

10. _ _ P _ R I M _ _ _ (a test or trial to make a scientific discovery)

RUNNING REPAIRS

Repairs are important on a spacecraft. In this puzzle FOUR items, which have NINE letters in their names, have been broken up into blocks of THREE letters, and the blocks have become completely muddled up. Can you come to the rescue and put the words back together again?

S P A	U I T	T E L
U T E	O P E	I T E
E S C	S A T	P A R
C E S	A C H	E L L

CIRCLE OF LIFE

Our planet is the only one that is known to support life. Life is the first answer in our circular grid. Each four-letter answer begins in a numbered space, so join the circle, write in your answers and come back to where you started.

1. It is found on our planet and known on no other.
2. Takes in food.
3. Drinks slowly, through a straw if you are in space.
4. In space, seeds are planted in special pillows. On Earth they are planted in _ _ _ _ .
5. Arrive back on Earth.
6. A record that plays music, like the Golden Record on *Voyager* 2.
7. The constellation Cancer is represented by this creature.
8. The Big _ _ _ _ marked the origin of the universe.
9. Game played by astronaut Alan Shepard on the Moon.
10. It powers a spacecraft.

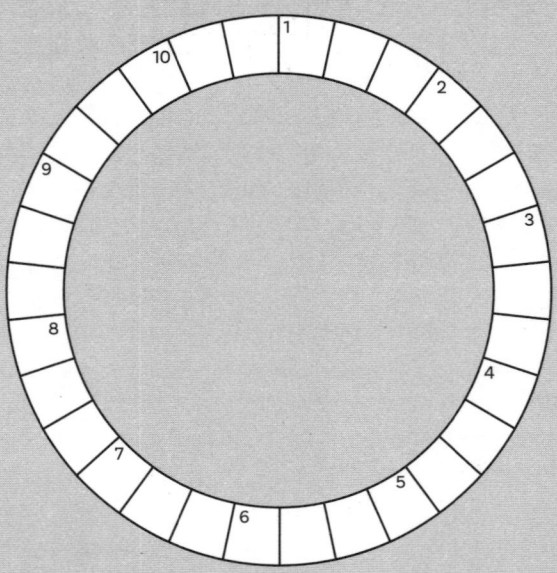

PLANNING IN STAGES

Planning is under way to build a spacecraft. Some of the sections are in place and they contain the number of days it took to build that section. The two numbers underneath a section when added together make the number above it. Fill in the blank sections showing how many days each section took to build. When you have finished the top section, your rocket is complete and will tell you how many days the project took. How many?

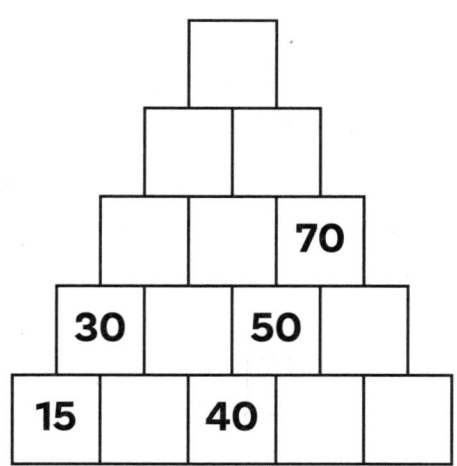

SPREADSHEET

Work is under way planning unmanned probes to study Jupiter, Saturn, Uranus and Neptune.

Various individual scientists, engineers and administrators are all spending time on the missions. Here's a sheet logging the hours that have been put in.

The first letters of the planets – J, S, U and N – are used to identify each project.

People have been asked to set a certain number of hours to each project. So, for example, if the figure for Jupiter was 15 hours, every J on the chart would stand for 15 hours. (Please note J does NOT stand for 15!)

There is a number at the foot of each column, reading down. These numbers are reached by adding together the hours spent on projects J, S, U and N in the column.

The numbers at the end of the rows are calculated in the same way. The final row has a question mark at the end. Can you work out which number should be there?

Tip: The third row features project J four times. That seems a good place to start.

J x 4 = 52

S	U	U	N	43
U	N	S	S	41
J	J	J	J	52
U	N	J	S	?
41	53	44	44	

FAST FORWARD

Fast-forward to the future in this puzzle where the middle letters of the words move forward in the alphabet. There are two clues in each case, and we give you the first answer.

1 Wins against someone else in a race * Bands of material in machinery

   BEATS   **BELTS**

2 Small sailing ships / Protective footwear

   _____   _____

3 Sound made when you press a switch / A timepiece

   _____   _____

4 An award made up of a disc hanging from a ribbon / Steel, iron or gold, for example

   _____   _____

5 The rungs on a ladder or stair / Puts an end to, ceases

   _____   _____

6 It prevents a vehicle from moving / Damaged something so it needed a repair

   _____   _____

7 The 'colour' of the hole in space where gravity is strong / Large piece of stone or ice

   _____   _____

8 A path / Ask the very good question, for what reason?

   _____   _____

TIM PEAKE

Perhaps the most well-known British astronaut is Tim Peake. Born in 1972, Peake began his career in the military, attending the Royal Military Academy at Sandhurst after leaving school. He showed exceptional skills in the army, rising through the ranks from lieutenant to captain in just a few years, and becoming a qualified helicopter instructor just four years after learning how to fly.

Peake would leave the military in 2009 after earning a degree in flight dynamics and evaluation and having achieved the rank of major – but new adventures awaited him. That same year, he beat over 8,000 applicants to earn one of six places in the European Space Agency's astronaut corps. A rigorous training programme followed, and in 2012 Peake became a NASA aquanaut when he spent 12 days at the Aquarius underwater laboratory – perhaps the closest experience to actual space travel that can be achieved without leaving Earth.

In 2015, Peake would finally realise his dream of going to space when he was assigned to the Principia mission aboard the International Space Station (ISS) – a mission that would see him spend almost 186 days in orbit. During that time, he would become the first British astronaut to conduct a spacewalk, and, in April 2016, became the first man (and second person after US astronaut Sunita Williams) to run a marathon in space when he took part in the London Marathon from the treadmill aboard t he ISS!

Peake's long stay in space ended in June 2016 when he left the station aboard a Soyuz spacecraft and returned to Earth. During his time in space he made approximately 3,000 orbits of Earth and travelled an incredible 78 million miles. Since retiring from his travels, Peake has written a number of books about his time in space and talks widely about his experiences as part of his role as an ESA ambassador, educating and inspiring the next generation of space explorers who will follow in his footsteps.

The *Soyuz TMA-19M* spacecraft that returned Peake to Earth is on permanent display at the Science Museum in London. It is the first flown human-rated spacecraft to be part of the museum's collection.

THE HUBBLE HOTEL

Welcome to The Hubble Hotel. This luxury hotel situated on the Moon is an ideal place for the holiday of a lifetime. All rooms have their own air supply along with a wet room, comprising a washing area and a toilet. There are lots of new and exciting packages on offer.

It's the year 2060. The Lightyear family are planning their first holiday staying on the Moon. There's Mum, Dad and the two children, 12-year-old Luna and her nine-year-old brother Astro. Which package will they go for?

ARMSTRONG ADVENTURE HOLIDAY:

Five-day break includes: All-day restaurant. Large family suite of three bedrooms. Free Space Buggy rides. Guided tours. All travel costs from Earth to the Moon and back.

GALILEO GETAWAY BREAK:

Seven-day break includes: Meals in the restaurant at set hours. Large family suite of three bedrooms. Use of a Space Buggy for the entire stay. Gymnasium. All travel costs from Earth to the Moon and back.

NEWTON BARGAIN BREAK:

Seven-day break includes: Large family suite of three bedrooms including kitchen area for self-catering. Space Buggy rides. Guided tours. All travel costs from Earth to the Moon and back.

APOLLO AMAZING ACTIVITY PACKAGE:

Fourteen-day break includes: 24-hour restaurant. One large family bedroom that sleeps four. Space Buggy rides. Top-of-the-range gymnasium. Daily guided tours. All travel costs from Earth to the Moon and back.

Mrs Lightyear does not want self-catering, but she would like use of a gymnasium.

Mr Lightyear wants to drive a Space Buggy.

Luna really wants her own bedroom.

Astro doesn't like guided tours.

The whole family wants at least a week on the Moon.

POINT UPWARDS

Each answer in the nose of the rocket pointing upwards has FOUR letters. The first letter goes in a numbered triangle, the second letter goes directly above it, the third letter goes to the right and the fourth letter goes to the left. The answer to No. 1 is IDEA. I goes in the numbered triangle, D is directly above it, E is to the right and A is to the left. Have you got the idea?

CLUES

1. Original thought, which might become a scientific theory.
2. Information, often numbers on a chart, to help scientists in space and on Earth.
3. Warmth inside the capsule.
4. Historic space base on the Florida coast, ____ Canaveral.
5. One movement in a spacewalk.
6. Month and day on calendar, to record a possible future launch.
7. Aircraft or sprays of water or gas.
8. Jupiter has a Great Red ____.
9. The countdown gets to here after 3, 2, 1.
10. A meteor is also known as a shooting ____.

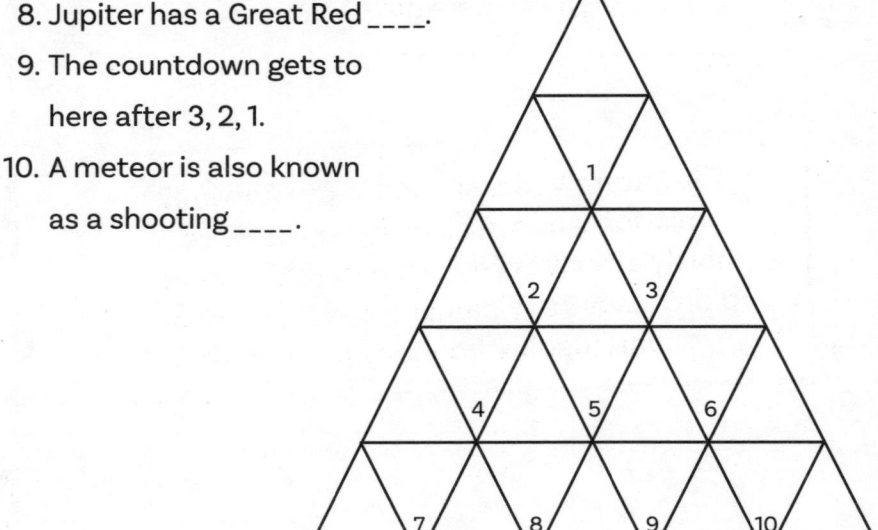

SPACE FACTS

The Space Shuttle is made up of over 2.5 million components, making it one of the most complex machines ever created!

Rockets are divided into stages that are jettisoned when they use up all their fuel. Most rockets have two to three stages, but some have up to five!

The Saturn V rocket used in the Apollo 12 mission was struck by lightning twice shortly after lift off! Fortunately, the strikes didn't cause any damage and the mission continued without any problems.

CROSSWISE

Words with a space link have had the letters in their names mixed up and rearranged in alphabetical order. Give the letters a spin and slot them in their correct numbered spaces in the square grid so that 4 across and the shaded letters going down give you two words which link to a trip beyond Earth's atmosphere.

1. C E M R R U Y

2. A E G O R V Y

3. A E E P P R R

4. I I M N O S S

5. D E L M O S U

6. E E L O P R X

7. E E M O R S T

SUNSPOTS

Scientists believe that the Sun still has more than 5 billion years of life left, so it will be around for a long time, way into the future. The words below all contain the letters in the word SUN, in the order S then U then N, but there will be other letters in between. Can you spot the correct words?

1. S __ U __ N __ __ (Earth's first artificial satellite) _____

2. __ __ U __ __ N __ (person at university who might study astronomy) _____

3. S __ U N __ (noise, such as the flames roaring from a rocket on take-off) _____

4. S __ __ U __ N (the planet with rings) _____

5. S __ U __ __ __ N __ (closing, as you would do with the hatch on the capsule) _____

6. __ __ S __ U __ N __ (saving someone from danger) _____

MYSTERY LETTER

Six sets of words with a space link are listed below. The letters in their names have been replaced by the letter Q. Each word also has a MYSTERY LETTER, which is the same throughout the puzzle, and is shown as the letter X. Can you work out the words and identify the MYSTERY LETTER? All the answers have appeared in the pages of this book.

1. Q Q Q X Q Q (Space vehicle)

2. Q Q Q Q Q Q X (Russian space vehicle)

3. Q Q Q X Q (Non-human space traveller)

4. Q X Q (Area with clouds)

5. Q Q Q X Q Q Q Q (A galaxy)

6. Q Q X Q Q Q Q (Leave Earth in a spacecraft or aeroplane)

LINE UP

Looking into the future, new planets may well be discovered. Planet A takes 200 Earth years to orbit our Sun. Planet B takes 400 Earth years to orbit our Sun. They both move in the same direction.

Planet A, Planet B and the Sun are all in a line.

How many Earth years will it take for the three to be in a line once again?

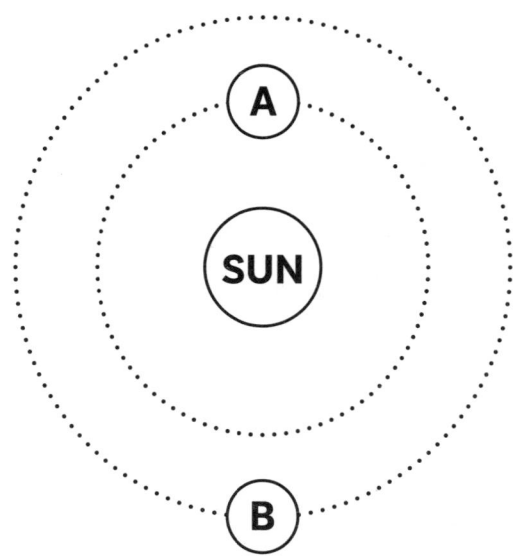

WHAT'S NEXT?

What's next in the lists?

31 28 31 30 31 30 31 ?

O T T F F S S ?

52 7 24 60 ?

M V E M J S U ?

S E L Z Z U ?

SPACE FACTS

Light years are used to measure vast astronomical distances. They are equivalent to around 5.88 trillion miles (9.46 trillion kilometres)!

The closest star to our Sun is Proxima Centauri, located 4.24 light years away. Travelling to this star using existing propulsion technologies would take thousands of years!

Did you know there's a sports car orbiting Earth? In February 2018, SpaceX launched a Tesla Roadster into orbit as a dummy payload for a Falcon Heavy Rocket. The car continues circling Earth, with a mannequin in a spacesuit called Starman behind the wheel and a copy of Douglas Adams' novel *The Hitchhiker's Guide to the Galaxy* in the glovebox.

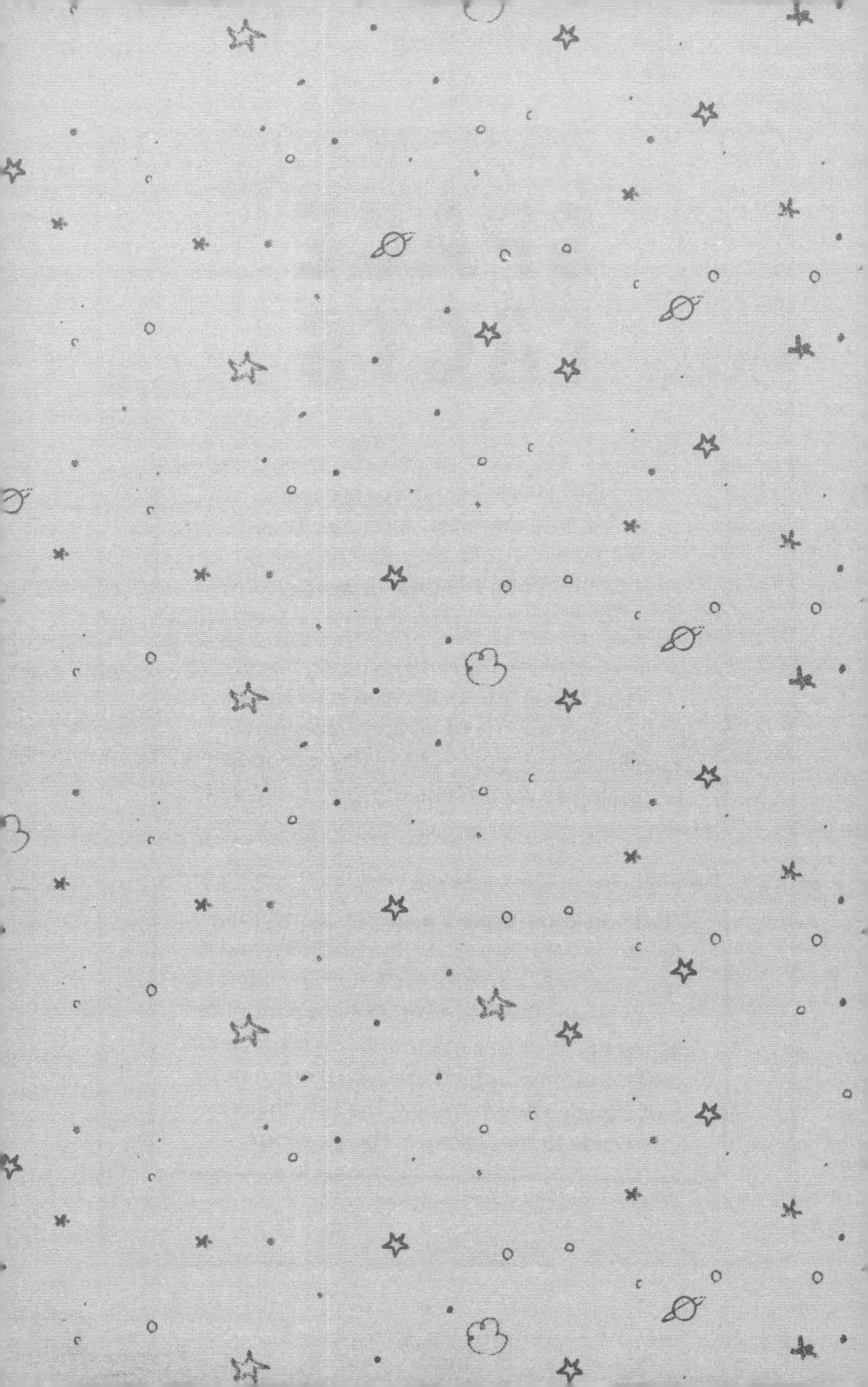

SOLUTIONS

CHAPTER 1

A BRIEF HISTORY OF SPACE

1. **WATCH THE SKIES!** Stargazer D has seen the most stars. A has seen 4 stars. B has seen 3 stars. C has seen 2 stars. D has seen 5 stars. E has seen 1 star.

2. **THE STUDY OF ASTRONOMY** 1. Star, 2. Ray, 3. May, 4. Stony, 5. Rats, 6. Moon, 7. Man, 8. Story, 9. Mars, 10. Tomato.

3. **IN ORBIT** 1. Race, 2. Pace, 3. Pack, 4. Pick, 5. Pink, 6. Rink, 7. Rank, 8. Rack.

4. **MAP IT OUT**

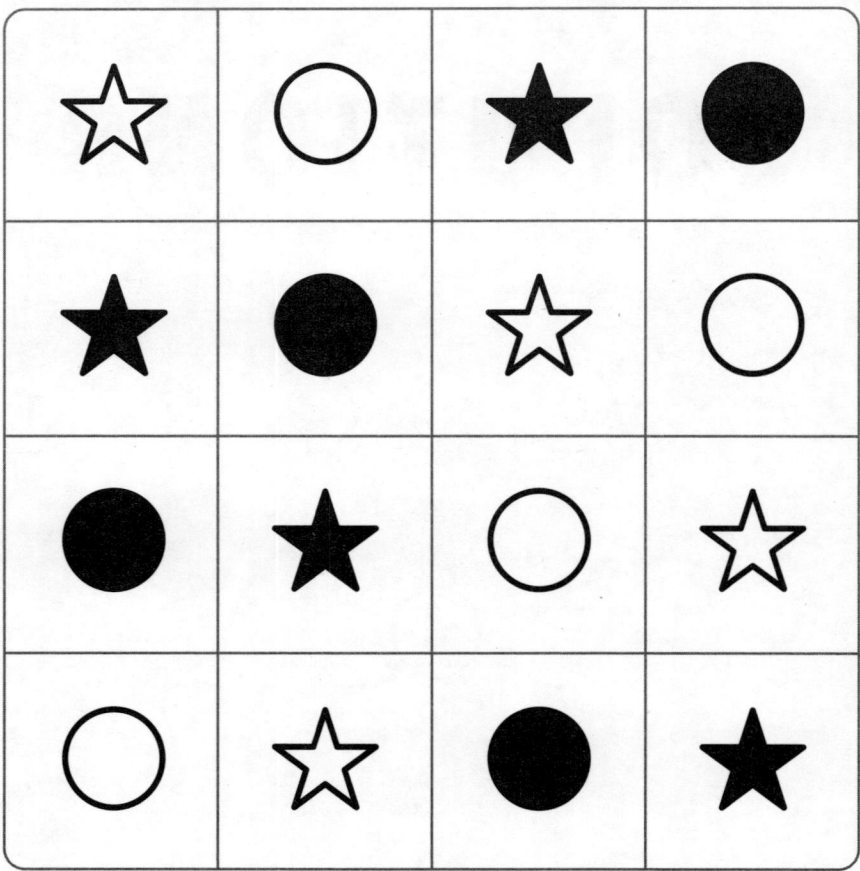

5. **CALENDAR CONUNDRUM** 1691, 1881 and 1961 read the same when you turn the numbers of the year upside down. 1609 is the odd one out.

6. **STARGAZING** Every straight line of four numbers totals 26.

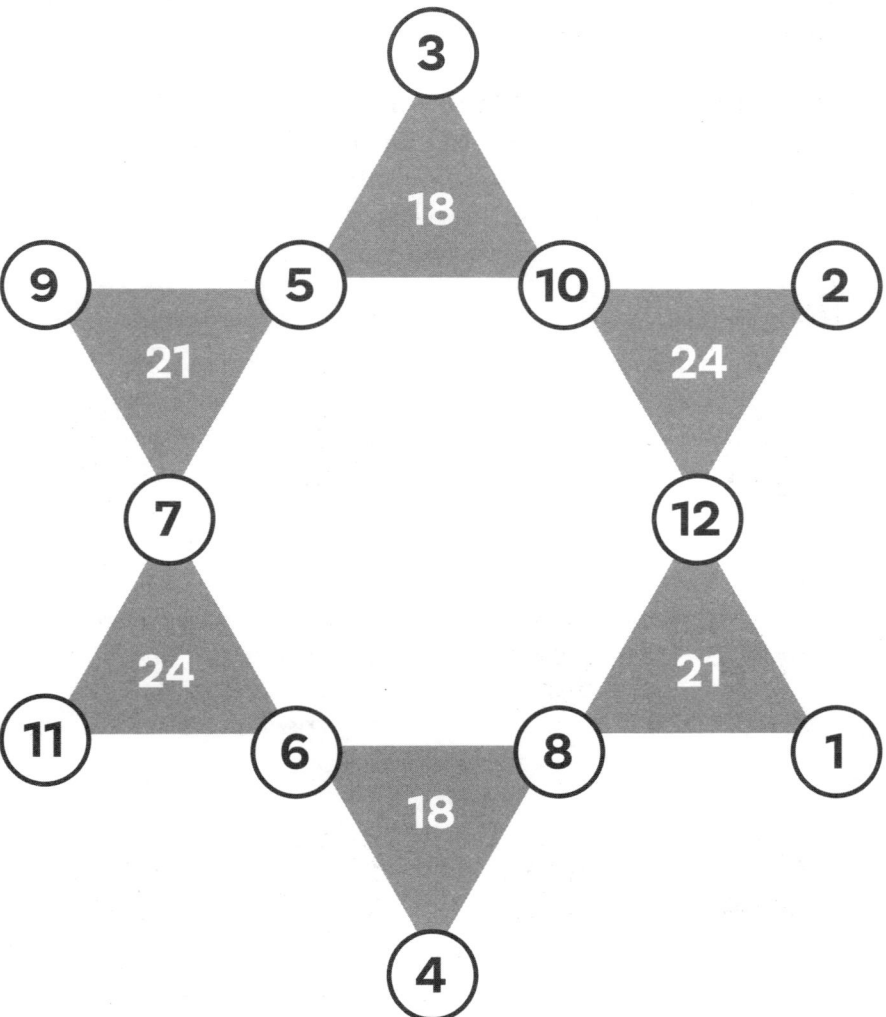

7. **ACROSS THE UNIVERSE** 1. Sun, 2. Saturn, 3. Star, 4. Venus, 5. Earth, 6. Comets, 7. Satellite, 8. Mars.

8. **SOLAR ECLIPSE** Top left: Rockets. Top right: Shuttle. Bottom: Satellite. The letter represented by the ? is T.

9. **TRUE OR FALSE** 1. True. He did say that, but the Sun is 1.4 million kilometres across, or 870,000 miles. 2. False. It was in fact an apple that he saw falling to the ground. 3. True. Something resembling a comet can be seen in the sky in the tapestry, but it wasn't named after Halley in the 11th century. 4. True. He wasn't believed by many people at the time because they thought Earth was flat. 5. False. The Great Pyramid of Cheops, which is considered to be the world's oldest observatory, is in Egypt and dates from 2550 BCE. 6. False. An interferometer is a type of radio telescope. 7. False. The first living creature in space was a dog called Laika. 8. False. Galaxy, Mars and Milky Way are the names of chocolate bars.

10. **CO-ORDINATES** 1. April, 2. Radar, 3. Miles, 4. Speed, 5. Touch, 6. Route, 7. Orbit, 8. North, 9. Glide.
The quotation is: 'The *Eagle* has landed', spoken by astronaut Neil ARMSTRONG when Apollo 11 landed on the Moon.

11. **MOONSTRUCK** The moons are exactly the same size. The positioning of the arrows creates an optical illusion that makes moon 1 look bigger than moon 2.

12. SPACE RACE

CHAPTER 2

PLANNING A MISSION

1. **PROJECT X** The project title is 'Is there life on Mars?'

2. **TEAMWORK** Hollie is an engineer who has worked for six months.
   Millie is a scientist who has worked for two years.
   Tim is an administrator who has worked for one year.

3. **FOLLOWING INSTRUCTIONS** Message reads: REMEMBER TO SAVE ALL THE INFORMATION THAT YOU HAVE KEYED IN.

4. **CODED PLANETS** Mercury has the highest total.
   1.Jupiter is 10 + 21 + 16 + 9 +20 + 5 + 18 = 99.
   2. Uranus is 21 + 18 + 1 + 14 + 21 + 19 = 94.
   3. Neptune is 14 + 5 + 16 + 20 + 21 + 14 + 5 = 95.
   4. Mercury is 13 + 5 + 18 + 3 + 21 + 18 + 25 = 103.
   5. Saturn is 19 + 1 + 20 + 21 + 18 + 14 = 93.

5. **ON TARGET**
   a) 1 + 25 + 75 = 101.
   b) 6 + 17 + 25 + 75 = 123.
   c) 4 + 20 + 75 + 400 + 500 = 999.

6. **PREPARING TO LAND**

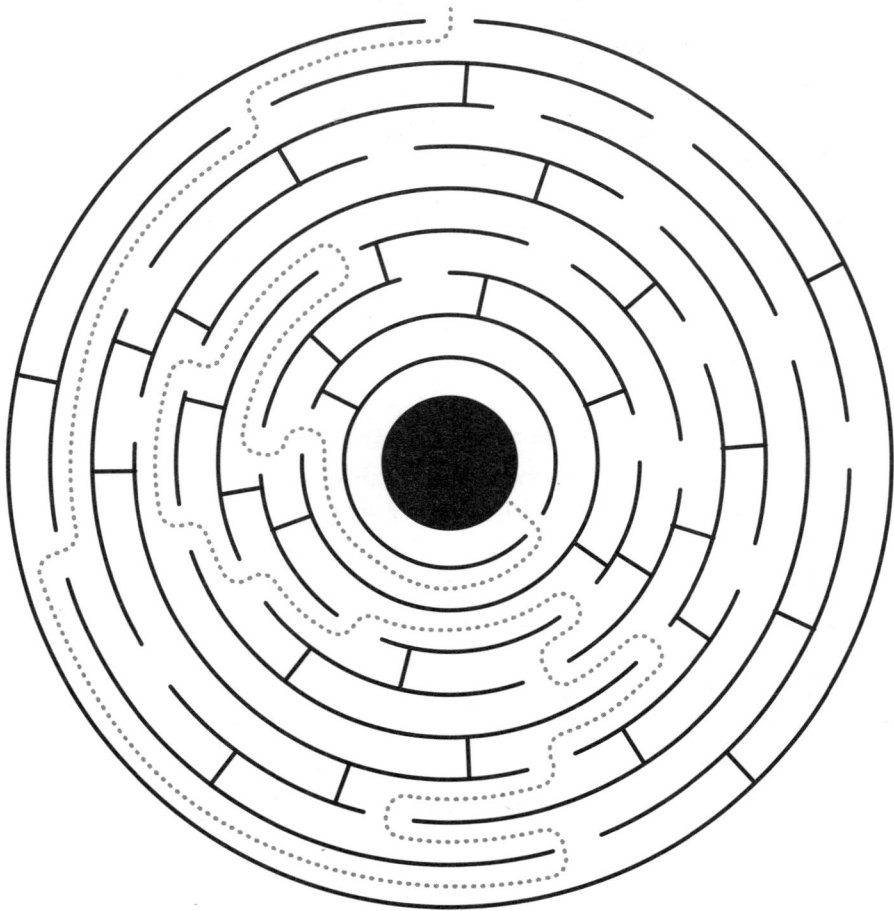

7. **BREAK UP** 1 Cloud, Stars, 2 Rocks, Stone, 3 Clock, Hours, 4 Crews, Teams, 5 Flood, Storm, 6 Journey, Travels, 7 Capsule, Shuttle.

8. **ALL SQUARE** 30 squares. There are 16 individual squares that are all the same size. These small squares can be linked in groups of four to form different larger squares. There are nine of these. The 16 individual squares can be linked in groups of nine to make even larger squares. They form blocks of 3 x 3. There are four of these. Finally, the outside lines enclosing the 16 small squares form one square itself. That gives 16 + 9 + 4 + 1 = 30.

9. **ENGINEERING** 1. Green, 2. Ring, 3. Energy, 4. Nearer, 5. Re-enter, 6. Designing, 7. Inner, 8. Beginning.

10. **CIRCUIT BREAKER**
    8 needs adding to circuit 1. $1 + 3 + 4 + 6 + 2 + 1 + 8 = 25$.
    5 needs adding to circuit 2. $2 + 8 + 1 + 1 + 4 + 3 + 1 + 5 = 25$.
    5 needs adding to circuit 3. $3 + 1 + 4 + 2 + 1 + 7 + 2 + 5 = 25$.

11. **STEPS IN SPACE** 1. Russian, 2. Compass, 3. Pacific, 4. Docking, 5. Ancient, 6. Gravity, 7. Celsius.
    The shaded squares spell out: ROCKETS.

12. **SHUTDOWN** 895. In attempt A, none of the numbers were correct. That means that every 3, 4 and 6 in other attempts must be in the incorrect place. Attempt B contains 3 and 4, and they cannot be in the correct place. There is one digit that IS in the correct place. That has to be the 5. Attempt C contains 3 and 6, and they cannot be in the correct place. There is one digit that IS in the correct place. That has to be the 8. Attempt D contains one correct digit but it IS NOT in the correct place. The 6 and 4 cannot appear in the code. That leaves the 9 as the correct number.

    We already know that the first digit is 8 and the last digit is 5. That means 9 goes between them as the second digit.

CHAPTER 3

TRAINING TO BE AN ASTRONAUT

1. **ALL ACTION**
   The word that appears THREE times is SWIM.

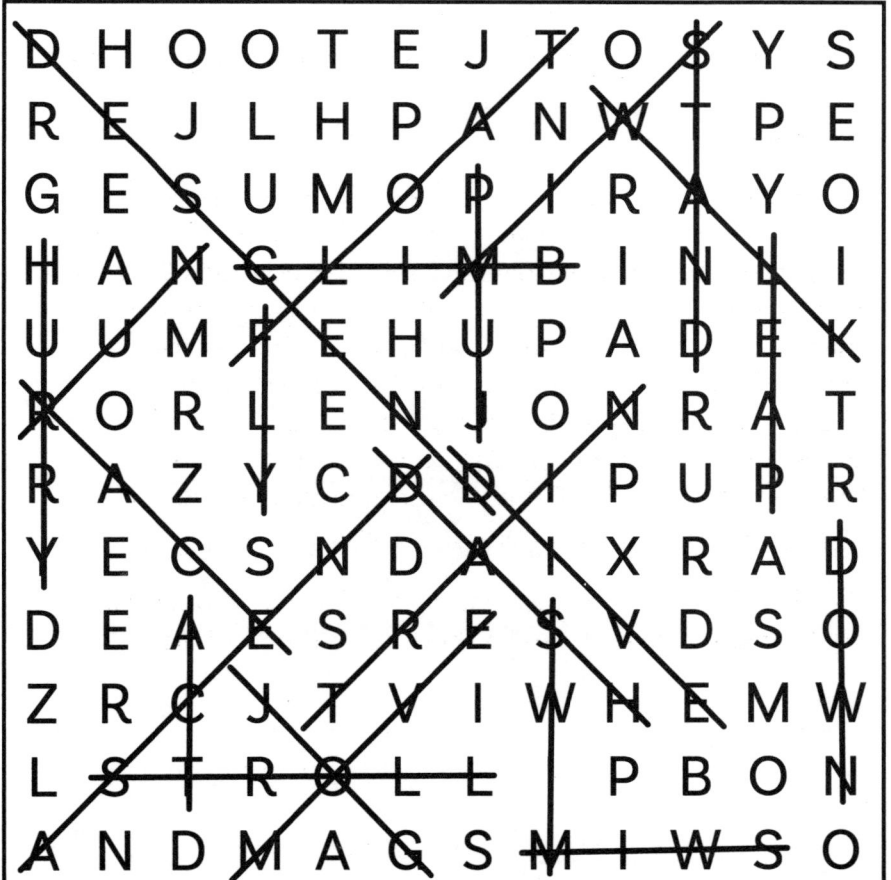

2. **INTERVIEW** The order is: Matt, Mila, Tim, Li. The alphabet clue tells us that Li was not first, so she was second, third or fourth. Matt was not second, so he was first, third or fourth. Mila was not third, so she was first, second or fourth. Tim was not fourth, so he was first, second or third. We are told that neither Tim nor Mila was first in, and that Tim went in after Mila. Tim cannot be first or second, and we know that from the alphabet clue he cannot be fourth. He has to be third. Tim was interviewed directly after Mila, making her second. That leaves the first interview and the fourth interview between Li and Matt. The alphabet clue means Li was not first. She has to be fourth, leaving Matt as the first. Now that's sorted, let's hope they all did well!

3. **NUMBER NAMES** MILA is code number 14. T = 1, M = 2, I = 3, A = 4, L = 5. The letters in TIM add up to 6. They have to be 1, 2 and 3. You cannot decide which letter equals which number at the moment, but you do know that letters A and L (letters not used in TIM) must be greater than 3. A is either 4 or 5. L is either 4 or 5. If A was equal to 5, then for MATT to equal 8, the letters M + T + T would have to equal 3. That would mean each of the letters would stand for 1 (1 + 1 + 1 = 3). That doesn't work, so A must stand for 4. Take away the A from MATT and that leaves the letters M + T + T = 4. That means M must equal 2 and T must equal 1. LI equals 8, with letter L = 5, leaving letter I as 3.

4. **SHAPE UP** Only box C contains all the parts to build the robot.

5. **TYPO** There is always excitement at the thought of TRAVEL to outer SPACE in a ROCKET. MAN has landed on the MOON but not on MARS. All astronauts need a helpful CREW behind the scenes. Some astronauts have been used to flying PLANES before they ventured beyond Earth. As part of their training they may live in CAVES, or in SNOWY WOODS. Sometimes they practise in TANKS full of water. They carry out TESTS and checks are made on their HEALTH. They must WEAR a special SUIT.

6. **JIGSAW**

7. **MAKING CONNECTIONS** 1. Ware, 2. Head, 3. Water, 4. Off, 5. Test, 6. Eye, 7. Down, 8. Land.

8. **LEVELS** Test tube E and test tube J have the wrong surface levels.

9. **SPACE PLACE** 17 and 6 are used to fill the empty spaces. The line now reads: 17, 11, 6, 5. The number far left has the second number taken away from it. This creates the third number. 17 – 11 = 6. In turn, the second number has the third number taken away from it. This creates the fourth and last number. 11 – 6 = 5.

10. **EYE, EYE** 1. CANCEL, 2. OPEN, 3. HELP, 4 .MENU.

11. **SCREEN SHOT** The two words remaining are: JINGLE and BELLS. JINGLE BELLS was the name of the first song transmitted from space to Earth in December 1965. 1. deletes IGLOO, FOOD and SOLO. 2. deletes TROUT (Tutor) and CHEATER (Teacher). 3. deletes DOG and MONKEY. 4. deletes EXTRA and FOXES (contain an X). 5. deletes CREW and TEAM. 6. deletes SINGLE, TANGLE and TINGLE.

12. **TESTING, TESTING** 1. Nowhere. If they were survivors they would still be alive and wouldn't be buried. 2 Incorrectly. 3. Both satellites, A and B, will be the same distance from Earth when they meet. 4. Three astronauts is the smallest number of astronauts in the line. Two in front of one, two behind one and one in the middle. 5. NOON.

CHAPTER 4

LAUNCH DAY

1. **COUNTDOWN** There is a total of 29 triangles. The cone of the rocket contains three triangles. There are two individual triangles plus one new triangle formed by joining shapes together. Each wing contains seven triangles. There are two individual triangles plus five new triangles formed by joining shapes together. The central area contains eight triangles. There are four individual triangles plus four new triangles formed by joining pairs of triangles together. There are four individual triangles on the lower part of the rocket. 3 + 7 + 7 + 8 + 4 = 29.

2. **TEN...** 1. Content, 2. Listens, 3. Often, 4. Extend, 5. Antenna, 6. Pretend, 7. Utensil, 8. Sentence, 9. Tent, 10. Tendon.

3. **NINE...** 1. Dried, 2. Icy, 3. Visor. The name of the Space Shuttle is *Discovery*.

4. **EIGHT...** 1. Universe (C), 2. Engineer (A), 3. Every day (A), 4. Einstein (C), 5. Asteroid (C), 6. Landings (C), 7. Journeys (C), 8. Selected (C).

5. SEVEN...

```
              A           R
          M I S S I O N
              R           C
              L           K
    J         O           E               S
  S U R F A C E     A T T E M P T
    P         K           S               U
    I                                     T
    T         I           D               N
  N E P T U N E     T R A N S I T
    R         N           R               K
              S           A
              T           W
              A           I
          C L O S I N G
              L           G
```

6. **SIX** ... 1. Travel, 2. Clever, 3. Create, 4. Stages, 5. Sounds, 6. Minute, 7. Simple, 8. Helmet, 9. Bright, 10. Airman, 11. Uranus, 12. Russia.

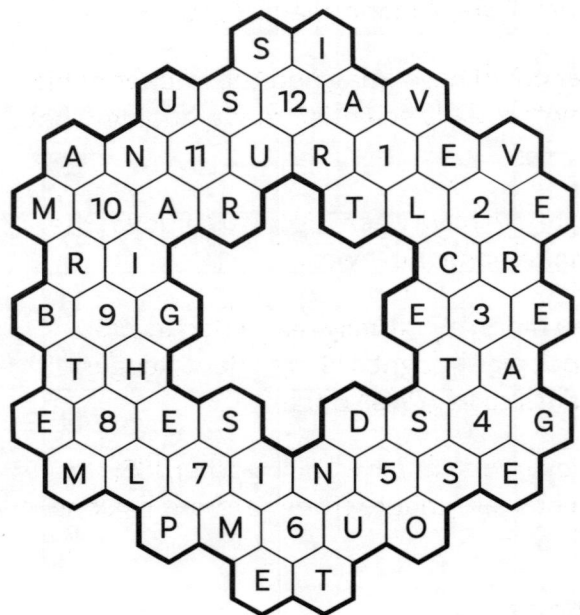

7. **FIVE** ... The missing planet is EARTH.

E	A	R	T	H
A	W	A	R	E
R	A	R	E	R
T	R	E	A	D
H	E	R	D	S

8. **FOUR** ... 1. Snow, 2. Wind, 3. Mist, 4. Gust, 5. Gale.

9. **THREE** ... The letters N, S and U do not appear. They can be used to spell out SUN.

10. **TWO** ... 1. Hear, Here, 2. Red, Read, 3. Sun, Son, 4. Weigh, Way, 5. Neil, Kneel, 6. Hours, Ours, 7. Plane, Plain, 8 Stair, Stare.

11. **ONE** ... Galileo never could have imagined the impact of his telescope. Isaac Newton, early scientist, made findings that are still used today.

    Planets and dwarf planets have been discovered down the ages, Pluto, Neptune to name but two.

    Putting a man on the Moon eventually happened in 1969, sooner than some people thought. US President Reagan phoned the astronauts to say, 'Well done!'

    On a space mission everyone must work together. ISS, the space station, even has astronauts from different nations working together.

    ONE appears NINE times.

12. **LIFT OFF!** 1. The nose cone changes size between images. 2. The band below the nose cone becomes wider. 3. Different number of stripes top of the wing, left. 4. Black area on the wing tip, right, changes shape. 5. Diagonal line changes direction on foot of the rocket.

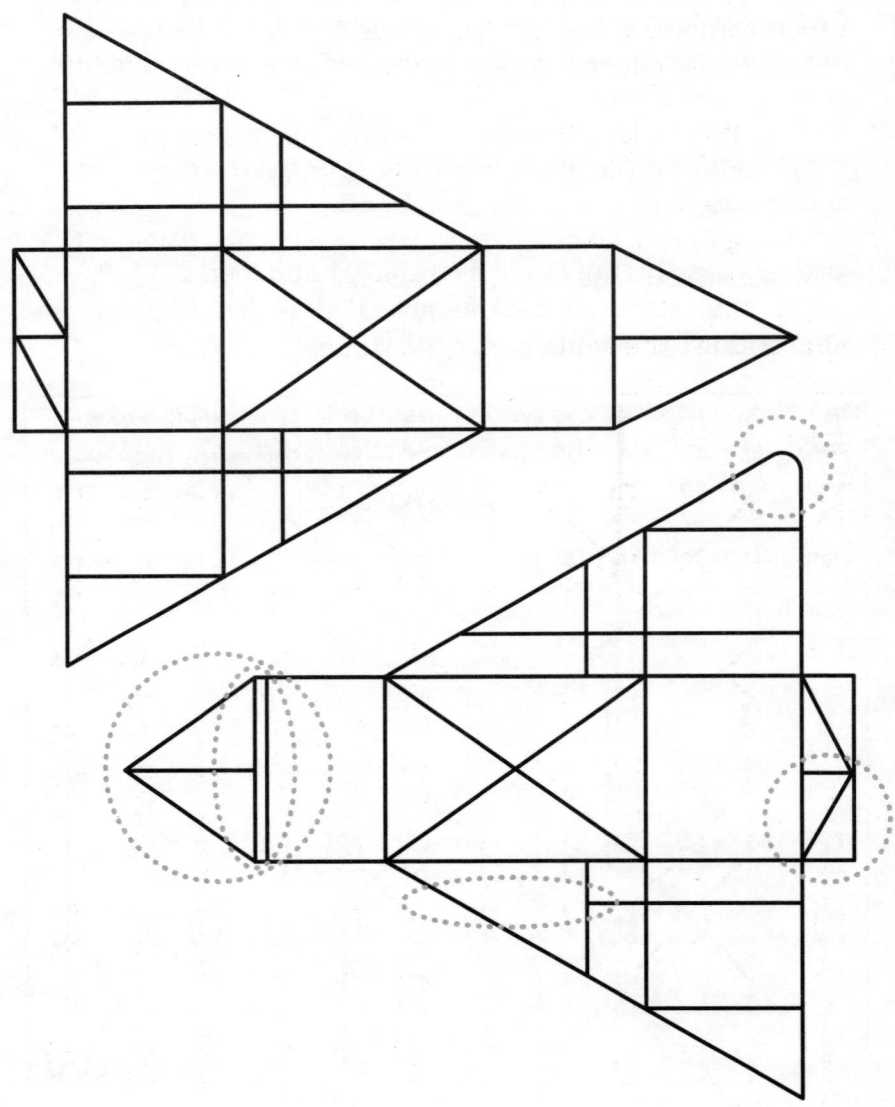

CHAPTER 5

LIVING IN SPACE

1. **QUOTE** 1. Tools, 2. Image, 3. Medal, 4. Power, 5. Earth, 6. After, 7. Knows, 8. Enter. The quotation is: 'Popping outside... for a walk tomorrow.' The astronaut was TIM PEAKE. His walk outside was, in fact a walk in space.

2. **RECYCLING** 1. Glass, 2. Paper, 3. Clothes, 4. Envelopes, 5. Cardboard, 6. Plastic, 7. Batteries, 8. Water bottles.

3. **Stick Together** 1. Airlock, 2. Cargo, 3. Countdown, 4. Launchpad, 5. Mealtimes, 6. Moonlight, 7. Spacesuit, 8. Sunrise.

4. **KEEPING FIT** The word you will not find is STRETCH.

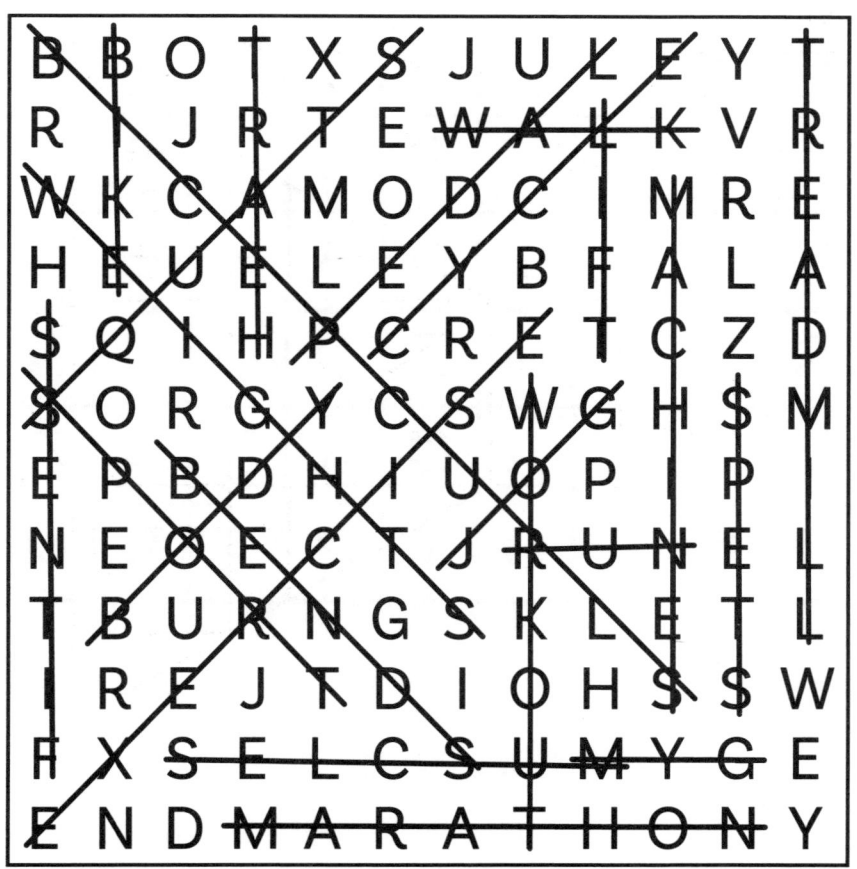

5 **THE BRUSH OFF** C, G, B, E, A, F, D.

6. **FABULOUS FOOD** 1. Chicken, 2. Cheese, 3. Crackers, 4. Cookies, 5. Ham, 6. Ice cream, 7. Tacos, 8 .Macaroni.

7. **KEEP IT TIDY** A2. C3. D3.

8. **ROCKETMAN**

T	A	K	E	C	M	N	R	O
E	M	N	R	K	O	C	T	A
C	O	R	N	A	T	E	M	K
R	C	O	T	M	E	K	A	N
N	E	A	K	R	C	M	O	T
K	T	M	O	N	A	R	E	C
A	K	T	M	E	N	O	C	R
M	R	C	A	O	K	T	N	E
O	N	E	C	T	R	A	K	M

9. **WATCH IT!** The line goes just below 10 and just below 3; 10, 11, 12, 1, 2, and 3 are in one half; 4, 5, 6, 7, 8 and 9 are in the other half. Both sets of numbers total 39 when added together.

10. **CUBE FOOD**

C	U	B	E
U	P	O	N
B	O	L	D
E	N	D	S

I	T	C	H
T	R	U	E
C	U	B	E
H	E	E	L

I	C	E	D
C	U	B	E
E	B	B	S
D	E	S	K

11. **MICROGRAVITY** 1. Spins, Snips, 2. Strap, Parts, 3. Mir, Rim, 4. Gas, Sag, 5. Star, Rats.

12. **THE FINAL STRAW** Take one of the straws from the equals sign. Place it diagonally on the left of the plus sign to turn it into a number 4. The new sum reads 141 – 11. That gives the answer 130. Well, we did say it was a trick!

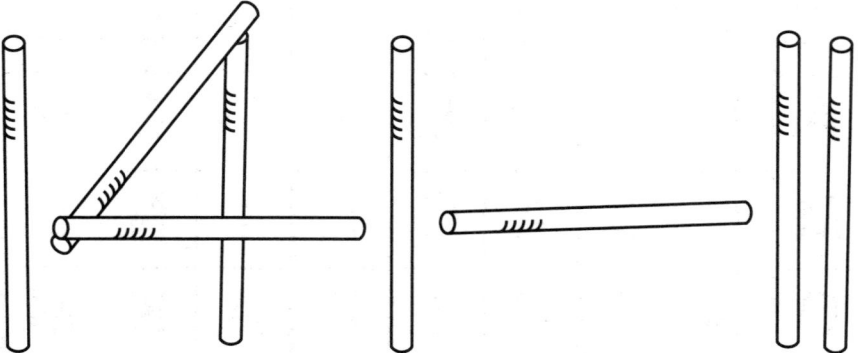

CHAPTER 6

SCIENCE IN SPACE

1. **DATA TRANSFER** GREAT RESULTS.

2. **ORBITS**

A. 243. Multiply each number by 3. 1 x 3 = 3. 3 x 3 = 9. 9 x 3 = 27. 27 x 3 = 81. 81 x 3 = 243.

B. 10. Each number is halved. It is divided by 2. 320 ÷ 2 = 160. 160 ÷ 2 = 80. 80 ÷ 2 = 40. 40 ÷ 2 = 20. 20 ÷ 2 = 10.

C. 65. The two digits in the numbers are reversed.

D. 3,600. Multiply each number. The multiplying digit gets greater with each move. 5 x 2 = 10. 10 x 3 = 30. 30 x 4 = 120. 120 x 5 = 600. 600 x 6 = 3,600.

E. 13. Think of the numbers written as words. The pattern is the number of letters in the word. 1 is written as ONE and is the lowest number containing three letters. 4 is written as FOUR and is the lowest number containing four letters. 3 is written as THREE and is the lowest number containing five letters. 11 is written as ELEVEN and is the lowest number containing six letters. 16 is written as SIXTEEN and is the lowest number containing seven letters. The next number is the lowest number containing eight letters. The answer is 13 written as THIRTEEN.

3. **PLANT POWER** Day 13. If the plant doubles in size every day, the container will be half-full the day before day 14.

4. **STEPS** 1. Air, 2. Pair, 3. Paris, 4. Praise, 5. Parties, 6 .Stripe, 7. Trips, 8. Tips, 9. Sit.

5. **MOVING ROBOTS** Yes. Robot A made one move to his left then stopped. After all the movements, Robot B finishes one move to the left from his original starting position.

6. **FACE FACTS** 1. Nose, 2. Eyes, 3. Ears, 4. Teeth, 5. Eyelashes, 6. Eyebrows.

7. **ALL CHANGE** 1. Heat, Head, Held, Hold, Cold. 2. Land, Hand, Hard, Herd, Here.

8. **SEEING DOUBLE** GRID A: Clues across: 3 Check, 6 Hold, 7 Sleep, 8 Peas, 10 Raced, 14 Dish, 15 Cloud, 16 Mend, 17 Twins. Clues down: 1 Ships, 2 Clear, 4 Helped, 5 Crew, 9 Saturn, 11 Dives, 12 Shade, 13 Flew.
GRID B: Clues across: 3 Earth, 6 Walk, 7 Diary, 8 Ants, 10 Ocean, 14 List, 15 Outer, 16 Shoe, 17 Blink. Clues down: 1 Sweat, 2 Pluto, 4 Animal, 5 Turn, 9 Screen, 11 Night, 12 Steel, 13 Fuel.

9. **SHAPE UP** 4 and 5.

10. **BOXING CLEVER** 24. A cube has six sides or faces. Imagine each side had a different number of dots on, like a dice. The six-dot side is at the top of the cube, so it can be seen when placed in the box. Keeping the six on top, the cube could be taken out of the box and put back in a different position four times. It could face north, south, east or west. That is true for each of the six sides. 6 x 4 = 24.

11. **MIXED MENU** 1. Save, 2. File, 3. Share, 4. Edit, 5.Insert, 6. Set up, 7. Select, 8. Clear, 9. Paste, 10. Draw.

12. **PASSCODE** The digits in the middle row are 14   10   6. This is the PASSCODE. The completed square looks like this:

12	2	16
14	10	6
4	18	8

CHAPTER 7

EXTRA-TERRESTRIAL LIFE

1. **SHADOW PLAY** 1. Clock, 2. Pause, 3. Venus, 4. Hatch, 5. Error, 6. Flame, 7. Straw, 8. Rhyme.

1	2	3	4	5	6	7	8
C	A	N	H	E	A	R	Y
O	U	S	C	R	E	A	M

The quotation is: In space, no one ... can hear you scream! It is from the movie *Alien*.

2. **WHO AM I?** MARTIAN

3. **STRANGE SIGNS** The strange signs are in fact numbers. Each number combines with its mirror image to the left, producing the unusual shapes. The top row reads 5 3 1 6. The middle row reads 8 0 7. The bottom row reads 9 4 2. When the numbers are added up, each row totals 15.

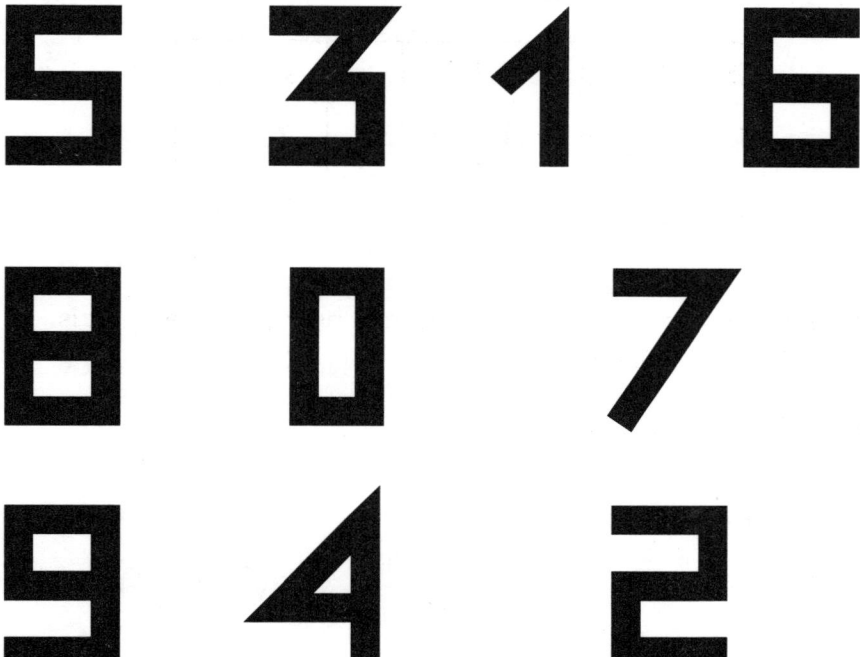

4. **THE MAN IN THE MOON**
   E has the highest total.
   A. 0 + 0 + 0 + 1 + 2 + 2 + 6 = 11.
   B. 0 + 0 + 1 + 3 + 3 + 4 + 8 + 8 = 27.
   C. 0 + 2 + 3 + 4 + 4 + 5 + 8 = 26.
   D. 0 + 0 + 0 + 3 + 6 + 7 + 9 = 25.
   E. 0 + 0 + 2 + 6 + 6 + 7 + 7 = 28.
   Did you remember the 0s?

5. **UFO** 1. Uniform, 2. Buffalo, 3. Suffolk, 4. Unfortunate, 5. Unfolded, 6. Underfoot, 7. Bullfrog, 8. Unfroze.

6. **MYSTERY MESSAGE** The message reads: I AM AN ALIEN. The first number, 8, has to be I, as you would not have a K on its own. In 17, the first letter must be A and only M could follow it. It's a similar pattern for 16, A, and N. It could have been AT but this wouldn't have made sense when you finished the sentence. Alien has the letters under 8 and 9 where there are just two choices, I or K for 8 and O or L for 9. To make a word that exists, 3 has to be E, and 6 has to be N.

7. **ALIEN TERRITORY** Journey 1. Take Yttrium from the danger area D to safe area S. It will be safe to leave Zirconium and Xenon together.
Journey 2. Return to the danger zone on your own.
Journey 3. Bring Xenon to the safety area leaving Z in the danger area – for now.
Journey 4. Bring Yttrium back to the danger area as it's not safe to leave Yttrium with Xenon.
Journey 5. Yttrium remains in the danger area alone as you take Zirconium back to be reunited with Xenon.
Journey 6. Zirconium and Xenon stay in the safe area while you venture back to the danger area to collect Yttrium.
Journey 7. You and Yttrium make the journey back to the safe area S. Phew, made it!

8. **EXTRA LINK** 1. Ozone, Neptune, 2. Meteor, Orbit, 3. Sun, Universe, 4. Jupiter, Terrestrial, 5. NASA, Saturn, 6. Astronomer, Mercury, 7. Earth, Theory, 8. Observe, Venus.

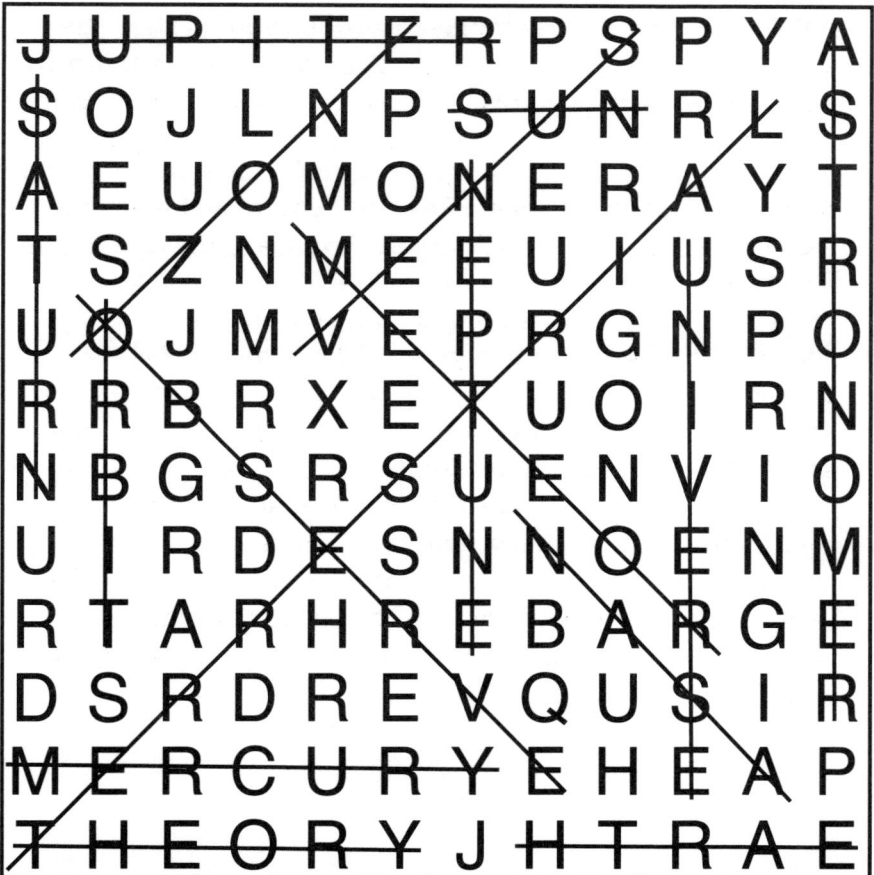

9. **THE VISITORS** Harry's alien was Phobos who could turn invisible.
   Jade's alien was Ganymede, who could read minds.
   Lewis's alien was Smosh7, who could fly.

10. **CIPHER FROM SPACE** The message reads: FRIENDS, CAN YOU READ OUR MESSAGE? HAVE WE GOT IT RIGHT? This is the code:

A=26	B=25	C=24	D=23	E=22	F=21	G=20
H=19	I=18	J=17	K=16	L=15	M=14	N=13
O=12	P=11	Q=10	R=9	S=8	T=7	U=6
V=5	W=4	X=3	Y=2	Z=1.		

11. **ODD ORDER** The titles all contain numbers that are written out as words. Each word appears as a line of consecutive letters. ONE appears in title 1. TWO appears in title 2. THREE appears in title 3. FOUR appears in title 4. FIVE appears in title 5.

12. **PLANET PROBES** 1. Mars, 2. Saturn, 3. Uranus, 4. Neptune.

CHAPTER 8

WHAT'S NEXT?

1. THE COSMOS

2. **LUNAR LOTTERY** Girl A is Star, whose ticket is 999. Boy B is Leo, whose ticket is 360. Girl C is Venus, whose ticket is 237. Girl D is Miranda, whose ticket is 730. Boy E is Ray, whose ticket is 307. Add the numbers on each ticket together and the lowest number is 9 on Leo's ticket 360. Leo is the winner!

3. **TEXT TRICKSTERS** 1. Touchdown, 2 .Sunrise, 3. Back to Earth, 4. Lost in space, 5. Over the Moon.

4. **NEXT, PLEASE!** 1. Planet, 2. Neptune, 3. Universe, 4. Oxygen, 5. Engineer, 6. Telescope, 7. Newton, 8. Einstein, 9. Expedition, 10. Experiment.

5. **RUNNING REPAIRS** The FOUR items are: PARACHUTE, SATELLITE, SPACESUIT, TELESCOPE.

6. **CIRCLE OF LIFE** 1. Life, 2. Eats, 3. Sips, 4. Soil, 5. Land, 6. Disc, 7. Crab, 8. Bang, 9. Golf, 10. Fuel.

7. **PLANNING IN STAGES** The project took 365 days – a whole year!

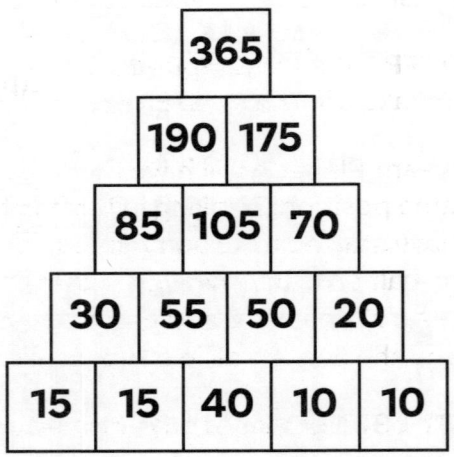

8. **SPREADSHEET** 46 replaces the question mark. N = 15. J = 13. U = 10. S = 8. The third row shows that J x 4 = 52. Divide 52 by 4 to find that J = 13. Row two contains the letters U, N, S and S. The column on the far right contains J, N, S and S. The only differences are the letters U and J. J = 13. The total for the column is 44, the total for the row is 41. This means U has to be three less than J. 13 – 3 = 10. In the column far left you now know the value of J, U and U (13 + 10 + 10 = 33). The column totals 41, so S must be the difference: 41 – 33 = 8.

9. **FAST FORWARD** 1. Beats, Belts, 2. Boats, Boots, 3. Click, Clock, 4. Medal, Metal, 5. Steps, Stops, 6. Brake, Broke, 7. Black, Block, 8. Way, Why.

10. **THE HUBBLE HOTEL** The Galileo Getaway Break meets all the requirements of the family.

11. **POINT UPWARDS** 1. Idea, 2. Data, 3. Heat, 4. Cape, 5. Step, 6. Date, 7. Jets, 8. Spot, 9. Zero, 10. Star.

12. **SUNSPOTS** 1. *Sputnik*, 2. Student, 3. Sound, 4. Saturn, 5.Shutting, 6. Rescuing.

13. **CROSSWISE** 1. Mercury, 2. Voyager, 3. Prepare, 4. Mission, 5. Modules, 6. Explore, 7. Meteors.
The shaded letters going down spell out CAPSULE.

14. **MYSTERY LETTER** 1. Rocket, 2. *Sputnik*, 3. Laika (a dog), 4. Sky, 5. Milky Way, 6. Take off. The MYSTERY LETTER is K.

15. **LINE UP** 200 years. Planet A will have made a full orbit and be back in the same position. Thinking in terms of a clock face, planet A will have started at 12 and moved back to 12. Planet B will have made half an orbit. Thinking in terms of a clock face, planet B will have started at 6 and has now moved to 12. The two planets and the Sun are all in a line once more.

16. **WHAT'S NEXT?** 1. 31. Number of days in calendar months starting with January. Seven numbers are given. August is next as the eighth month of the year. It has 31 days.
2. E. They are the first letters of numbers. One, Two, Three, Four, Five, Six, Seven with Eight the next in order.
3. 60. Measuring time on Earth. 52 weeks in a year. 7 days in a week. 24 hours in a day. 60 minutes in an hour. 60 seconds in a minute.
4. N. They are the first letters of the planets in order of distance from the Sun. Mercury, Venus, Earth, Mars, Jupiter, Saturn, Uranus and then Neptune.
5 P. Spells out PUZZLES reading backwards.

First published in Great Britain in 2024 by Seven Dials,
an imprint of The Orion Publishing Group Ltd
Carmelite House, 50 Victoria Embankment
London EC4Y 0DZ

An Hachette UK Company

1 3 5 7 9 10 8 6 4 2

Text © SCMG Enterprises Ltd 2024
Puzzles © The Orion Publishing Group Ltd 2024
Puzzles written by Roy & Sue Preston
Biographies and Space Facts by Tim Leng
Chapter texts by Heather Bennett
Artwork by us-now.com

A CIP catalogue record for this book is
available from the British Library.

ISBN (Trade Paperback) 978 1 3996 2389 6
ISBN (eBook) 978 1 3996 2390 2

Designed by us-now.com
Printed in Great Britain by Clays Ltd, Elcograf, S.p.A

www.orionbooks.co.uk